"Ciment's book is a frank and refreshing discourse on art and artifice, and the unexpected path of an authentic life."
—*Colorado Springs Independent Review*

"A page turner. . . . One woman's journey into the 'heart of darkness' and back, or perhaps beyond."   —*Jerusalem Post*

"This is a beautifully written novel. Ciment transported me to another world where both art and dignity matter. Fantastic!"
—Alice Sebold, author of *The Lovely Bones*

"Start to finish, *The Tattoo Artist* is rich in Ciment's trademark wit, intelligence, and gorgeous prose. I shall not soon forget this story."   —Lynn Freed,
author of *The Curse of the Appropriate Man*

"Jill Ciment's new novel, like her previous books, is beautifully written and reaches even beyond them as a stunning work of the imagination. I read *The Tattoo Artist* on one long plane ride, totally immersed and fascinated."   —Howard Zinn,
author of *A People's History of the United States*

JILL CIMENT

THE TATTOO ARTIST

Jill Ciment was born in Montreal, Canada. Her books include two novels, *Teeth of the Dog* and *The Law of Falling Bodies*; a collection of short stories, *Small Claims*; and a memoir, *Half a Life*. She has been awarded two New York State Foundation for the Arts Fellowships and a National Endowment for the Arts Fellowship. Ciment is a professor of English at the University of Florida. She lives in Gainesville, Florida.

THE
TATTOO
ARTIST

THE TATTOO ARTIST

JILL CIMENT

Vintage Contemporaries

VINTAGE BOOKS

A DIVISION OF RANDOM HOUSE, INC.

NEW YORK

The Library of Congress has cataloged the Pantheon edition as follows:
Ciment, Jill, [date]
The tattoo artist / Jill Ciment.
p. cm.
1. Tattoo artists—Fiction. 2. New York (N.Y.)—Fiction. 3. Women travelers—Fiction.
4. Women artists—Fiction. 5. Castaways—Fiction. 6. Tattooing—Fiction.
7. Oceania—Fiction. 8. Islands—Fiction. I. Title.
PR9199.3.C499T37 2005
813'.54—dc22
2004061215

Vintage ISBN-10: 1-4000-7844-X
Vintage ISBN-13: 978-1-4000-7844-8

Book design by Virginia Tan

www.vintagebooks.com

For Arnold

PART ONE

CITY OF COFFINS

Yesterday, on the corner of Broadway and Fifty-seventh Street, a perfect stranger introduced himself to me and said, "I just want to tell you how very brave I think you are." I was about to flee on foot (no small feat at my age), when the stranger qualified his statement, "I mean, you've done nothing to disguise yourself, you look just like your photograph in *Life* magazine. Desecrated."

Another time, another stranger came up to me in the lobby of my hotel and, without prelude or warning, touched my cheek. "How could you have done this to yourself?" the woman asked. "Please tell me it washes off."

The tattoos that most disturb people are the ones on my face. There's no way of getting around them. There's no way of asking me, "Ma'am, you think the Yankees will take the pennant?" or "Mrs. Ehrenreich, do you believe that Bauhaus furniture is coming back into fashion?" without the tattoos turning the cordial exchange into a mockery of chitchat.

That is the point. That's the reason for their existence.

They begin on my cheeks and work their way down, covering every inch of me—my lips, tongue, throat, breasts, hips, thighs, even the soles of my feet. Though I didn't actually do all the procedures myself (How could I have? The pain renders one insensible), I am responsible for their design; all except for the tattoos on my face. As for my facial tattoos, I am more than responsible; I am culpable. But I'm getting ahead of myself, and you don't even know what my tattoos look like. They are not your usual crude sailor's fare, though to give credit where credit is due, I did incorporate a certain garishness, a seaman's vulgarity, into some of the imagery. Nor are my tattoos the intricately patterned signature of the Ta'un'uuans, the Michelangelos of South Sea tattooing, though once again, certain traditions have been alluded to. No, my tattoos, like all my art, are mine and mine alone, and herein lies my need to steel myself before revealing them to you. To have to endure one's own art, to be covered by it twenty-four hours a day, seven days a week, seeing every flaw over and over again, or worse, every act of unnecessary bravado, is simply unbearable.

My tattoos, like all the tattoos of my island, are a pictorial narrative, an illustrated personal history, though not necessarily a chronological one. Time as you know it, modern time with its clocks and calendars, has no place on my island. The location of each vignette is determined by the body, and how much pain a particular limb or bone or muscle can withstand, and how much agony, or pleasure, a particular event caused the subject. And this is where the true art of Ta'un'uu's tattooing comes in. The artist must not only create a suitable image to embody a crucial ordeal, or victory, she must also find a suitable place for it on an ever changing, forever decaying canvas.

To fully appreciate my story, you must view my tattoos in their entirety, front and back, every square inch of me at once, including the crumpled skin and sagging muscles upon which my tattoos are engraved. The islanders believe the way a body ages is as vital to the final design as the imagery. They believe that age is the final patina of art. This is why the modern world can't bear to look at me. I mean, really look at me. They can ask, "Mrs. Ehrenreich, do you consider yourself a cargo cultist?" "Mrs. Ehrenreich, what does it feel like to be back in the modern world after thirty years as a castaway?" They can say, "Sara, we just want to tell you how very brave we think you are."

But look at me?

No.

CHAPTER ONE

I was born in 1902 on the Lower East Side, that open sore on the hip of Manhattan. My parents had immigrated to America the year before from a *shtetl* outside Warsaw. The Ta'un'uuans have taught me, however, that a journey never begins at the point of departure, but at the point of origin, and so I envision my parents, neither taller than five feet, my father's face bewildered and terrified, my mother's, arrogant and terrified, fleeing the pogroms of Russia for the pogroms of Rumania, Rumania for Budapest, Budapest for Warsaw, Warsaw for Antwerp, and finally arriving at a cold-water flat on the Lower East Side. My parents were not only exhausted by the journey, they were stupefied. In the end, the only question that truly preoccupied them was one that, in my bohemian youth, I dismissed as greenhorn sentimentality, and now, in old age, is the only question I, myself, ask: Where is home, and how do I get there?

Like the children of most fresh-off-the-boat Jews, I attended the only school my parents could comprehend, let alone afford: a landsman's quasi Hebrew school conducted in a cellar and lorded over by a succession of rod-wielding, self-appointed rabbis. My education consisted primarily of chanting Hebrew songs without having the least notion of, or reverence for, what I was singing.

The islanders believe that language originates in song, and that the human throat is a musical instrument, a flute of flesh and blood, and that the breath reverberating through the flute is the soul, and that the music emerging from the flute is the spirit.

Aside from a few deeply ingrained Hebrew songs, everything else has been lost to me from those years. I have, after all, been gone so long. The only keepsake I have is an ancient newspaper clipping, a gift from the archivist at the Yiddish Library who'd read about me in *Life:* it's a 1916 "Bintel Brief," the advice column of the *Jewish Daily Forward,* in which a letter of my father's was printed.

Dear Esteemed Editor,

I hope you will advise me in my present difficulty. I come from a small town in Russia, where, until I was twenty, I studied the Torah, but when I came to America, I quickly changed. I was influenced by progressive newspapers, and became a freethinker and a socialist. But the nature of my feelings is remarkable.

Listen to me: every year when the month of Elul rolls around, when the time of Rosh Hashanah and Yom Kippur approaches, a melancholy begins to eat at my heart, like rust eats iron. When I go past a synagogue during those days and hear the cantor singing, my yearning becomes so great I cannot endure it. I see before me the small town, the fields, the little pond, the *yeshiva.*

I recall my childhood friends and our sweet childlike faith. My heart constricts, and I run like a madman till the tears stream from my eyes and I become calmer.

Lately, I have returned to synagogue, despite the scorn of my freethinker daughter. I go not to pray to God, but to hear and refresh my aching soul with the cantor's melodies. I forget my unhappy weekday life, the dirty shop, my boss, the bloodsucker. All of America with its hurry-up life is forgotten.

What is your opinion of this? Are there others like me whose natures are such that memories of their childhood songs are sometimes stronger than their convictions? I await your answer.

Respectfully yours,
Benjamin Rabinowitz

I offer you my father's letter not to woo you with nostalgia, but because if there were an untouched square of skin left on my body, I would engrave it on my flesh.

Jewish law forbids tattooing: Thou shall not make in thy flesh a scratch over the soul. But what if the Ta'un'uuans are right, and the soul is breath? Then aren't the scratches left on my soul by my needles really just the moments when my breath caught, my voice cracked, unable to find song?

By sixteen, I had become, in my father's words, a freethinker, and by my own definition, a bohemian and an anarchist, a girl for whom religion and its trappings were irrelevant. To bring the point home to my parents, I would invariably light my after-dinner cigarette in the flame of the Sabbath candles.

I was a seamstress by day, a waist maker, the eighteenth girl in a row of twenty at the windowless end of the warehouse. Shopgirls worked their way toward the light by seniority. By week's end, my fingers would be so scratched and marred by the needles that one can't attribute all the abrasions on my soul to the tattoos. But on Saturday nights, I'd don my shopgirl's version of bohemian—a felt hat with purple plumage, a Gypsy skirt, and two immoral shanks of red stocking. My destination was Greenwich Village. The cultural gulf between the Lower East Side and Washington Square was probably greater than the one my parents had encountered when they left the steppes of Russia for Avenue D. At best, I'd covet a bench at the base of Stanford White's arch, sharing cigarettes with versions of myself, gaudily feathered shopgirls in whose discontented stares one could just make out little compressed diamonds of ambition. At worst, I'd wander the square by myself, catching glimpses of what anyone could plainly see were the real bohemians— paint-splattered artists, mustachioed socialists, regal-necked poetesses arguing away while ash spilled from the gold tips of their cigarette holders. The schism between them and me in my red stockings and cheap plumage, seemed as impossible to surmount as that between the gods and man.

For shopgirls like me, East Side Jews who spoke with guttural accents, the only lifeline out of workaday hell was the Educational Alliance, the center of Yiddish intelligentsia, a curious mix of night school, public forum, gymnasium, and revolutionary cells. The center had been a gift from a few philanthropic German Jews to their hardscrabble East European brethren. Sunday afternoons, young Zionists who could barely remember to water their mothers' rubber plants took to the stage to call for the transformation of an arid desert into a Jewish

Eden. Ex-*yeshiva* shopboys, for whom the threading of a sewing machine was a daunting task, called for a futuristic mechanized utopia on earth.

My union, the Ladies' Waist Makers' Union, bought blocks of tickets for the Alliance's Sunday night lecture series: "Jews and the Graven Image"; "Is Marxism Scientific?"; "Revolution: If Not Now, When? If Not Us, Who?"; "The Jewish Themes of Ibsen."

One evening, an artist, an American Jew who had been educated in Zurich and Berlin, who had lived in Paris and Moscow, who spoke with intimacy about Picasso, Freud, and Trotsky as I might gossip about the girl at the next sewing machine, addressed us waist makers, and the boys from the Buttonhole Makers' and Collar Makers' unions, on the twentieth-century collision between art, the subconscious, and revolution.

A giant of a man, he had to stoop to reach the lectern. He had shoulder-length blond hair that he tossed to make his points. In a buckskin jacket and red silk vest, he dressed, to my mind at least, like a cross between Buffalo Bill and what I assumed was a Parisian painter. He told us that the art of the future would be made by the proletariat, workers just like us, then described the squalor of our shop life in enough glorious abstraction that it actually seemed possible. He explained how our subconscious, the antechamber of our unconscious, held within its misty foyer all the symbols we'd ever need. He urged us to have faith that art, with its noble and redemptive powers, would use those symbols to provide our beleaguered souls with the metaphors by which we could transform our misery into meaning. And when the time was right, he insisted that art would even spur us into revolution.

Did I believe him? A ragtag army of seamstresses and ex-*yeshiva buchers* advancing on Park Avenue brandishing needles and Symbolist paintings? What was the alternative? Fifty more years at a sewing machine? A tiny air shaft apartment facing a teenier one, my only view my neighbor's life? Whimpers, moans, hacks, grunts, fits of coughing, fits of prayer resounding through the thin walls? On the Lower East Side, the unconscious was not the symbol-laden fog of Freud and art. The unconscious was sleep or, if it lasted long enough, death.

Whatever doubts I had about his lecture I quickly quashed, as one might instinctively step on a dark shape in the periphery of one's vision.

When he climbed off the podium, I and a dozen other shopgirls surrounded him. He glanced down at us with bemused curiosity and teased us that his lecture would be followed by an impromptu quiz. He reached into the fringed pocket of his jacket and plucked out a gold cigarette case. Tapping his thumbnail on the tooled casing, he asked if any of us ladies would like to try a French cigarette? I was the only one to accept. I leaned into his lit match as defiantly as I leaned into the Sabbath flame. The rumor was that when he'd lectured at the Alliance the year before, he'd bedded only the prettiest of his admirers, comely girls with dreams as fragile as soap bubbles, girls who giggled at his rarefied allusions as others might nervously guffaw at a funeral. I wasn't particularly pretty, and I never giggled.

It would be easy to pretend that after thirty years among the islanders with their forthright sexuality, their worship of the body, I've lost all tolerance for the curtsies and bows, the feints and feigns of Western courtship. But even as a young woman, I detested coyness. Suffice it to say, when the other girls dispersed, it was I who followed him home, and I who seduced Philip.

His portrait graces my left breast. It is the first tattoo I engraved on myself. The portrait, however, in no way resembles the face I kissed that night; an unlined, untested face of cavalier certitude that the future would be as easy to read as a palm. The face on my left breast is desecrated, pillaged of all illusions, and though it breaks my heart to admit it, it is also the weakest part of my design—the point on my flesh where my emotions exceeded my skill—and no amount of virtuosity can disguise that weakness. The face on my left breast is a living death mask, as far removed from the young Philip as I am from the girl I was.

He lived in a refurbished livery stable on Washington Mews, refurbished with Carrara marble, Art Nouveau windows, Persian carpets, a Brancusi bronze, a gilt-framed Gauguin, and a collection of South Pacific masks. I was so ill educated, I didn't even know enough to be impressed. I thought the masks were examples of modern art. I walked up to the Gauguin and asked if Philip had painted it. When he laughed and shook his head, his hair whipped against his throat. I was too embarrassed to ask anything else. Just to end my ungainly silence, I unbuttoned my blouse and put my own collateral on display. I could see how amused he was by my brazenness. I was hardly amused; I was astounded by my daring. I let him finish the job, undoing the buttons, eyelets, hooks, and laces that confined me. I was and I wasn't a virgin. I'd had rudimentary sex the month before with a buttonhole maker on the Alliance's tar roof. Afterward, the boy and I declared ourselves freethinkers and never spoke to each other again.

Philip made love to me on his Hindoo blue settee. A practiced and precise lover, he believed his sojourns into the subconscious, his experiments with what he called "Surrealism," had led him to new levels of sensuality. I was hardly prepared to be the judge of that. I was still learning how to kiss.

I stayed with Philip for three nights and two days. He introduced me to the practice of automatic drawing after sex. With him, I tasted my first glass of champagne, my first bite of *trayf.* But what impressed me most, what trumps all my other memories despite half a century, is that Philip owned a telephone, an elegant black instrument on a fluted pedestal. I'd never seen one in a private house before. Whenever it rang, Philip grew exasperated, but I felt we were at the center of the world.

When I finally returned home, my frantic mother demanded to know where I'd been, and when I shamelessly told her, she called me a *nafka,* a whore, and wouldn't speak to me. The logistics of our not talking in a two-room tenement were complex. We had to steal past each other without so much as our breaths mingling. I had to bear witness to her mumbled quips without so much as a snipe back. Only my father, who had begun residing more and more in the bucolic fantasy of his Russian childhood, would speak to me. And only when my mother wasn't home.

"Sara, do you see that wall?" He had taken to believing that not only our tenement, but the sweatshop, his boss, all of America with its hurry-up life, was only a figment of his dreams. "That wall isn't a wall. That wall is the inside of my coffin." He took out his *tefillin* and prayer shawl, then kissed my cheek. "But you're not to worry, *mein kint,* I'll soon wake up."

I packed what little I had and left him *davening* toward the east, an air shaft strung with laundry, singing what must be the most heartrending of prayers, "Thank you God for returning to me my soul, which was in Your keeping."

I found lodging with six Litvak sisters from my union in a cellar apartment on Ludlow Street. My bed was the board that covered the kitchen tub. All night long, directly under my ear, the faucet leaked in fits and dribbles. My dreams sputtered and raced in time to that watery metronome, save for the nights that I slept beside Philip.

I wasn't his only lover: he made that unequivocally clear. He also made the conditions of my spending the night in his bed as complicated as a wedding contract. I couldn't stay for more than three consecutive nights. I couldn't keep any of my possessions in his closets or drawers. I was never to answer the telephone, though when it trilled, I pined to.

He practiced what he called "free love," the unrestrained taking of lovers, which he patiently explained to me was the logical culmination of being a freethinker. He believed that sex was one of the few connecting links of the human with the divine. He saw bourgeois marriage as the ultimate subjugation of the spirit, an economic union at best, a form of bondage at worst, having nothing to do with passion. He spoke about idyllic South Seas societies outside Western capitalism, islands of free love, where sex was a form of prayer. Of course, he granted me the same freedom to take as many lovers as I wanted, encouraged me to, in fact, though I couldn't imagine whom I'd bring home to my tub.

Besides, I didn't want anyone else. Watching him perform even the most workaday tasks—crushing out a cigarette, the way a tributary of blue veins appeared on his forehead when he was trying to make a point, the sheer dimensions of him as he stooped through a Victorian doorway— absorbed the whole of my attention. His shoes were as large as shoe boxes. He tasted of French tobacco and English port, whereas my buttonhole maker had tasted of herring and cheap vodka. He bought me a vermilion silk turban, which he claimed all the bohemian ladies were sporting. He automatically included me in their number. At five feet tall, even wearing my turban, I barely cleared Philip's elbow, but he didn't seem to mind. He had me parade naked before him at the foot of his bed. He had me lie perfectly still while he shut his eyes and touched me all over. He called it "a sexual offering." Whenever his hands momentarily paused, I felt something within me grow taut. I was still unformed in those years, little more than romantic ectoplasm waiting to be molded, and Philip seemed eager to give me shape. I could sense how intrigued he was by the idea of transforming a shopgirl into a revolutionary, a *shtetl meydel* into a bohemian. I could feel his excitement. It was as close as I had ever come to having power over someone, and I equated it with love.

I caught a fever one night and couldn't go home. When I tried to get up, Philip's bedroom floor seesawed, his hallway folded up like the bellows of an accordion. I could hardly navigate my way to the bathroom, let alone through the streets of New York. Philip made me lie down again and sponged me with alcohol. He used cotton swabs to cool the whorls of my ears. He insisted I drink tea laced with whiskey.

When I started to shiver, he made love to me. He gave me pen and paper, and asked me to draw my fever dreams. Even racked with chills, even under the sway of Philip's unshakable belief that the future of art lay with the masses, I didn't think my shopgirl visions were worthy of depiction. So I drew my father's visions instead. I drew a city of coffins—coffin skyscrapers, coffin sweatshops, coffin els streaking past coffin tenements— and within each and every coffin room, I drew my poor, *davening* father with shekels taped over his eyes. When I finally put away the pen, Philip looked down at my drawing with the same rapt awe he bestowed on his mask collection, on his Gauguin. He said, or I hallucinated that he said, "If I could draw like you, *mein lieb,* I'd will myself a fever every second of my life."

My temperature spiked and troughed for a week. When it finally abated, Philip cooked me soft-boiled eggs and rice. He insisted I remain in his bed for another few days, lest my fever come roaring back. He bathed me in a concoction of rose water, lemon, and soap, then changed my damp bedding for the tenth time. I luxuriated in his fastidious caretaking. I was in no rush to recuperate. Without so much as a word spoken between us, I simply never left.

On the bottom of my right foot is tattooed a plain wooden coffin. Jews do not believe in extravagant death rites. Thou shalt not be shamed, no matter how poor, by the simplicity of the shroud or box in which thou is buried. The coffin, however, is not for my father, who died that winter in the great 1918–1919 influenza pandemic, nor is it for my bereaved mother, who followed him shortly afterward. The coffin, the plain wooden vessel of a coffin, is reserved for my own voyage home.

CHAPTER TWO

The body provides such a limited canvas that the tattoo artist can't afford to squander even an inch of flesh to commemorate the trivial. That is, of course, provided that the artist can distinguish between the trivial and the important. At eighteen, had I been offered my body as a canvas, I might have covered myself with the lovesick doodling of a shopgirl. This is why the Ta'un'uuans don't allow their young to be tattooed, why they insist that the soul must be marked before the body.

Philip had grandiose plans for us, for me. He orchestrated my initiation into the fledgling New York art scene with the bohemian equivalent of a debutante's coming out. He persuaded Gertrude Vanderbilt Whitney, champion of the avant-garde and heiress to the Vanderbilt fortune, to exhibit my coffin drawings at her Eighth Street salon, then invited everybody who was anybody to attend. When I arrived at my own reception on Philip's arm, wearing the clothes he had picked out for me (including a feather boa just vulgar enough to suggest my working-class origins), I saw what looked like marble goddesses in ropes of diamonds and financiers in pince-nez scrutinizing my poor *davening* father.

"Don't let them intimidate you," Philip whispered. "Diamonds can't buy what you have." In tails and scarlet cummerbund, he ushered me through the crowd. "Besides, they want to be provoked, Sara," he assured me. "That's why they've ventured downtown."

Then, in his hobnail boots (Philip always wore workingmen's boots with formal attire), he climbed up onto Mrs. Vanderbilt's Chippendale table to the shock and titillation of the ladies, and the contempt of their husbands, and gave an impassioned lecture that shoehorned me into art history. He said I was the next enfant terrible. He said I was America's great avant-garde hope. He left boot marks on the cherry inlays. He tossed back his long hair so fervently that it almost got caught on the chandelier. By evening's end, he had managed to wedge me into Modernity between Picasso and Duchamp.

Why would such an ambitious young man be so willing to subjugate his own strivings for a shopgirl like me?

The only child of a wealthy banker, Philip had been raised to expect the full assortment of life's possibilities, and from that glut of opportunity, he had chosen, to his father's disdain and his mother's alarm, the life of a revolutionary artist.

Philip revered art as other men revere money, or war.

If art is nothing more than the shadow of humanity, then Philip could divine life where others saw only a blur of abstract shapes. He could recognize art in the tiniest mote of being, intuit it in the mundane. He could proselytize until even the dullest cretin would feel the shock of art's intimacy. Philip could do everything but create art. Next to the Gauguin in his house, his own attempts at painting looked like feeble carbon copies, the visions of a man who is hopelessly gazing in the wrong direction when the spectacle occurs. When Philip drew the human figure, the result looked like a manikin. When he tried his hand at Cubism, the outcome was a dime-store jigsaw puzzle.

For a man who could patiently spend hours tracing with his fingertip the contours of my body, he rendered the female nude without subtlety.

In the foyer of his Mews home hung a small gallery of his early landscapes—Cubist forests, Futurist utopias, Fauvist seascapes. Over the years, Philip had changed isms as often as other men change socks. To walk past these paintings was like walking past a row of foggy windows through which the outside world is reduced to conjecture and theory. It was as if Philip could only render the massive shapes of art history, whereas painting requires the particulars.

By the time Philip and I met, he called himself a Dadaist, but in truth, he hadn't been able to get himself to go into his studio in more than a year, hadn't been able to get himself to produce so much as a single drawing in more than two.

The Ta'un'uuans have taught me that one's ability to create beauty is only commensurate with one's knowledge and acceptance of suffering, that art and pain are wed. If the islanders are even partially right, then at eighteen, I knew nothing about Philip's suffering, and even less about why he was unable to make art.

My exhibition was, in the rarefied world of Greenwich Village, 1920, a success. I sold work to . . . really, does it matter? Suffice it to say, with Philip's help, my drawings now hung beside Matisse and Sargent in the parlors of Park Avenue. By the time the exhibit came down, I fancied myself an artiste, and Philip fancied himself my collaborator.

He called us "conspirators in art's revolution against bourgeois rationality." He said, "Sara, you'll make the bombs, and I'll plant them in the houses of the rich."

Under his tutelage, we experimented with what he called "psychic automatism" by having me—us—drink absinthe as if it were tea, smoke "tea" as if it were tobacco. When the milky green liqueur had tugged us both into the netherworld, I would get down on the floor in Philip's studio and kneel over an enormous piece of paper that he had laid out for me, while Philip handed me supplies—a bamboo pen, or a piece of Pitt charcoal, or a camel-hair brush. Then, hunkering down beside me, he would place his hand lightly over mine, in the fashion of a hand on a Ouija pointer, and whisper softly into my ear, in the fashion of a hypnotist, the symbols that were to spin out of my pen. His hand was huge and concealed mine so completely that it often looked as if it were he who was drawing.

"*Mein lieb,* draw for me an egg in a birdcage." "A child's nightmare." "Convulsive beauty."

And I would render, with hallucinatory precision, the imagery I saw on the backside of my lids.

When the drug induced a state of hyperbolic eroticism, he would make love to me on top of the paper, all the while urging me not to cease drawing. And I would draw self-portraits—the convoluted path his hands took on my pelvis, say, or the pelvic bone itself as it resisted the weight of his body.

In the wake of these frenzied states, I'd lie stupefied in his arms, while he read aloud to me from Marx or Freud or Trotsky or Emma Goldman or Apollinaire. Philip was evangelical with his knowledge.

At some point during my radical education, though, I must have grasped the idea that Marx was trying to make, that if I did the actual labor, I should rule the means of production. At some point during my artistic awakening, I must have gleaned Apollinaire's heartfelt appeal to pursue my own version of reason. One evening, I instinctively wrenched my drawing hand free of Philip's grasp when he wouldn't quit trying to guide it.

He shot me a look of genuine bewilderment. "What are you doing?"

I pretended it was a mistake, but he knew it wasn't.

He got up, poured himself another absinthe, knocked it back. "What we have together is perfect. Why would you jeopardize it?"

Then he grabbed his coat and left. He didn't return until the next morning, and even then, he acted . . . if not cold, then numb. When we next attempted a "collaboration," I took my absinthe as if it were medicine, knelt over the paper, and feigned fervor and innocence, but Philip wasn't fooled. He remained on his feet, looking down at me from his enormous height. He didn't touch his drink, nor did he touch me.

"What are you going to draw tonight?" he asked.

I said I wasn't sure. I said, "Isn't the point of psychic automatism not knowing what you're going to draw."

"If you say so."

I picked up a pen. "All right, what should I draw, Philip?"

He didn't answer me.

"I said, what would you like me to draw?"

"I suppose whatever comes to your mind, Sara."

I dipped the pen into the inkwell and started spinning out my own visions. In no time, I covered the entire surface, saturating the paper with a deluge of imagery that I'd been saving up for months.

When I finally looked up, Philip hadn't moved. He was staring down at my drawing, like an acrophobic at a sheer drop. You see, all this time, Philip had honestly believed himself to be my daemon, the spirit that enters the body and guides the mortal to genius. I was the medium through whom he was finally able to create beauty, and here I'd filled up the whole sheet of paper without him.

He strode out of the studio, but I followed him this time. I said, "I thought you didn't believe in the bourgeois propaganda that art is created by lone individuals." I grabbed hold of his shirttail. I said, "I thought we were collaborators. Why should it matter which one of us does the grunt work?"

He reeled around and looked at me with such patent amazement that I was silenced. "You have no idea how much it matters," he said, and left.

Next day, we tried to act as if nothing had changed, but, of course, everything had changed. It was then that Philip started bringing home the women. At first, it was under the auspices of "varietism," the practice bohemian couples engaged in in order to overcome bourgeois jealousy and increase mental hygiene. We couldn't have been together more than six months when he brought the first one home. It wasn't to share, mind you. He brought her home to punish me for having completed a folio of etchings, etchings I made all on my own.

He showed up with her around midnight as I was pulling the last plate. She was mock society, nouveau riche, probably married to some shop boss turned millionaire. I think she was as surprised to see me as I was her.

She called me "missy" when Philip introduced us.

I called her "ma'am" and offered her my ink-stained hand.

Philip tried to steer her away from me and into the bed-room as quickly as possible, but I blocked their way. I hadn't grown up in the slums for nothing; I could steel myself when I needed to, rally bluster to conceal woe. I said, "Oh, Philip, don't hide your guest in the bedroom. Why don't you do it on the settee (I pronounced it "*sah*-teah") and let me paint you?"

Mrs. Nouveau Vanderbilt wasn't quite into practicing the mental hygiene she thought she'd wanted. She gave me a look of unabashed superiority, whispered something in Philip's ear, then left.

I think Philip was relieved to see her go. He feigned disap-pointment, but he could hardly conceal his excitement with the startling ramifications of my—how should I put it?—my offer. Next morning, he nonchalantly asked if I would have really gone through with it? Next evening, he wanted to know if I thought Munch's *Jealousy* was the quintessential painting about sexual madness, if I viewed Picasso's *Les Demoiselles* to be the final word on voyeurism? He worked on my burgeoning competitiveness. "Be honest with me, Sara. Do you actually believe Stieglitz's pretentious spiel about O'Keeffe's little water-colors being the sole voice of female sexuality?" By week's end, he had talked me into it.

Over the next three months, he brought home six different women and I produced six paintings. Five of the women were prostitutes, but the last one was a game socialite who had ven-tured downtown for the thrill.

As for the working girls, I instructed Philip to bed them, missionary style, on his Persian carpet. I myself was up on a stepladder, sketching. I wanted an omnipotent point of view, God's haughty and neutral angle. I wanted to eliminate deep space, vanishing points, all allusions to, and illusions of, reality.

The question, of course, is how could I bear to witness my love—and despite everything, Philip was my love in both eros and charity—bed another?

On the one hand, it was like watching Philip eat, or more specifically, masticate his food, swallow, shovel in another spoonful, chew, swallow, and so on and so forth. On the other hand, it was like watching all my illusions of being uniquely desired end.

As for the socialite, Mrs. Blanche "Binky" Whiting IV, I broke down and joined in.

Philip and I weren't even the most outrageous couple. In our little clique alone, painters and poets, anarchists and Trotskyites, exchanged lovers like letters. You must understand the times. Victorian mores had been obliterated in the Great War. Revolution felt imminent. No one knew what shape it would take. A heady effervescence for all that was new bubbled in the air. Even the Baroness Elsa von Freytag-Loringhoven shaved her pubic hair for Man Ray's camera.

Philip didn't make an appearance in any of the final paintings. All his presence manifested was effect, his effect on the women's expressions as he made love to them, his effect on me as exhibited by my frantic brushstrokes. I painted close-ups of the women's faces in ecstasy, ennui, grimace, self-possession, supplication, and power. I finished with a self-portrait, jealousy. Mrs. Whiting wanted to purchase her painting (ecstasy), but I said I would only sell it as part of the group.

I could have stopped the experiments whenever I chose. I could have begged Philip to be kind, and Philip would have been kind—not faithful, but kind. I could have rerouted our love, as a river is rerouted, so that it never overwhelmed its fragile levees. But I didn't. I was young, ambitious, untrained, naïve, and I had just been given a clue to what the islanders so profoundly understand: that art and pain *are* wed.

In the spirit of the avant-garde, I took the concept as far as it would go. I made Philip's infidelities my muse and, in turn, my muse created Philip's infidelities.

One evening, about three years down this well-trod path, Philip brought home a woman, a girl really, fresh from the factories. She was very Irish, very pretty, very young, but that wasn't the point. Up until then, Philip had been seeing a Muscovite poetess, and before that, a French sculptress, and before that, the always willing Mrs. Blanche "Binky" Whiting IV. But this girl was different. This girl was from the streets. She was my potential replacement.

I said, "Oh, Philip, you must introduce us."

Philip reluctantly made the introduction, and the poor girl curtsied. She called me "ma'am."

I asked, "Are you a union girl?" knowing full well she wasn't, that the factory bosses had been hiring Irish scabs to break up the so-called "Jewish-Bolshevik" conspiracy.

The girl glanced up at Philip, then shook her head no.

I said, "Really, Philip, you'd put your prick before your politics?"

The girl looked flummoxed, then petrified, and I hated myself and Philip for that. When she ran out the door, I had Philip follow her.

To punish him, I cut the right sleeve off his every Italian suit, his every silk shirt, his Japanese kimono, even his infamous buckskin jacket. Why the right sleeve? Why not?

To get back at me, he brought home another factory girl.

In return, I went after his Breuer chair with a sculptor's chisel.

By the time our little melodrama was over, we were sitting on orange crates and wearing rags. There wasn't a shred of anger left in either of us. We were too exhausted, and unnerved. Not by the loss of a shirt, a chair. We were, after all, Marxists. No, what sobered us was the indisputable knowledge that, with the slightest turn of the chisel, the tiniest snip of the scissors, we could destroy, or worse, lose each other.

Those years can best be described by the titles of my paintings: *Convulsive Beauty. Philip and Sara with Firmament. Philip and Sara with One Head. Self-Portrait Without Vanishing Point. Still Life Without Life. Varietism.*

The Ta'un'uuans never assign a name to a work of art. When the Christian missionaries told them that God's first creation, Adam, had been given the task of naming all His other creations, they wept for Adam. To them, Adam had been given the insufferable job of robbing the world of transfiguration, of impulse, of its potential to forever change. Adam had frozen existence by naming it.

The tattoo on my left ankle is of a stick man and a stick woman. I wanted Philip's and my youthful indiscretions distilled to the most elementary icons. I didn't want them taking up any more precious space than they justly deserve. The icons are very small, but size isn't as important as location. The islanders may not assign a name to a piece of art, but they so artfully assign a scale of pain to every body part. The ankle is notoriously painful, and is usually reserved, in island tradition, for a first love, or a first battle, or both. The Ta'un'uuans know that ankles invariably swell with age. This particular tattoo (you have to look very closely now) shows a man and a woman with their lips sewn together in a kiss, or in punishment.

It's hard to tell.

CHAPTER THREE

I was varnishing a painting when Philip came into the studio, took the brush out of my hands, and told me that his father had committed suicide. The year was 1929, and bankers were taking their lives with the casualness with which one takes an aspirin. Philip sank onto a paint-splattered stool, and, in a voice devoid of inflection, described how his father had showered and shaved that morning, put on a *yarmulke* and a formal shirt, a frock coat and silk tie—"he even put on garters with his socks, Sara"—then locked himself in his study and used a pistol from his glory days in the Hapsburg army. Philip said his mother had found him.

The result was odious. Months later, when I entered the study to retrieve a drawing of Philip's that Philip had given his father as a gift (the first he'd done in years), and which Mr. Ehrenreich had hung on the darkest, farthest possible wall, there was still an all-too-human stain visible on the frame.

Philip and his father's relationship had been based on mutual disapproval, though disapproval may be too neutral a term—disenchantment, really. When Philip was a boy, and Mr. Ehrenreich a young father, they had evidently been infatuated with each other to the exclusion of Philip's mother. But when the boy reached surly, carping adolescence, and the father became the object of the boy's tirades, Mr. Ehrenreich turned on his son as only a spurned lover can.

He sent the shy gangly boy off to Europe to be indoctrinated as he had been indoctrinated—German gymnasium, officer's commission, Swiss bank apprenticeship—fully expecting that when the young man returned, he would readily emulate his father, from his choice of claret down to the side on which he parted his hair.

Philip came back an anarchist, an avant-garde painter, an absinthe drinker with hair to his shoulders, and the scrimmage was on.

All this was to say that the money for the Breuer chairs, the Oceanic mask collection, the gilt-framed Gauguin, came from Philip's mother, a nervous, frail soul badgered into bitterness by her austere, acerbic husband. The money was part of her private inheritance, untouched and untouchable by Mr. Ehrenreich according to their old-world Jewish wedding contract. In the end, it hardly mattered. When the stock market plummeted, and Philip's father abdicated his life, her assets dwindled down to a single diamond necklace, three diamond brooches, and two gold wedding rings, which Mrs. Ehrenreich tied together with a black thread so that the larger one wouldn't accidentally slip off her skeletal finger and diminish her estate by a sixth.

With the biannual sale of a piece of jewelry, and a frugal lifestyle, there were just enough means for her to scrape by, but nothing left over for her son.

It was one thing to have theorized, over a glass of port,

the good riddance of wealth, to have debated, over brandy, the end of capitalism, to have known, as I knew, that having in abundance what others are in need of is wrong, and it's quite another to find oneself suddenly putting it all into practice.

As devastated as Philip was by his father's suicide, he also made a point to celebrate the end of capitalism. As soon as an acceptable period of mourning had passed, he threw an "end-of-the-world-as-we-know-it" bash. The gala's centerpiece was a four-foot-high pound cake that Philip had baked himself, then sculpted and frosted to look like the Chrysler Building. Wielding a Mexican revolutionary's machete that he had picked up at auction years before, he ceremoniously cut the skyscraper down to size, serving slices of gargoyles and office suites on paper plates to our anarchist comrades. Then, raising a glass overflowing with Russian vodka, Philip proposed a toast, "to the upcoming revolution," "to the dream made real," "to the end of opulence and greed."

I ate my cake and drank my vodka, but I forwent the toasts. You see, I had already known the other side of opulence, and I had no desire to go back there. In Philip's Marxist utopia, we all drank from the same glass. In mine, we all drank from the same crystal.

By my calculations, even if we sold the furniture and Philip's mask collection, we'd buy ourselves a year at most. Breuer chairs and Oceanic masks were suddenly out of vogue, as were the paintings of avant-garde artists.

I went back to the East Side to find work as a waist maker, but there wasn't any work, not even piecemeal labor. I banged on the gated storefronts of the Chinese sweatshops, but when they saw my American skin, they shooed me away.

For a time, I earned a pittance carving ice slugs for an ice-man on Rivington Street. The slugs sold three for a penny, and were used to feed the old tenements' coin heaters. When the gas man came to collect, all the evidence had melted. It didn't take long, though, for people to start carving their own.

I took in sewing. Even our bedraggled bohemian friends had to make their eccentric wardrobes last as long as they could.

Philip finally found us both work for a couple of months in a speakeasy, assisting an old academy painter with his mural, a scene of such ludicrous debauchery—Roman gods and god-desses on a Roman binge—that Philip couldn't help substitut-ing Hoover's face for Bacchus's. The Ta'un'uuans are smart enough to give their deities animal heads.

But the job that nearly undid me, that seemed to decimate the shaky calibrations of my own self-righteous principles, was the buying and selling of old gold. Only the most desperate souls partook of my services, and only after they had tried every-thing else.

I would knock on a stranger's door, the shabbier the door the better. Usually, the people inside were too frightened to answer. After all, I could have been a bill collector or a landlady. A couple of minutes later, hope would overtake reason, and a halting voice would ask, "Who's there?" After all, I could also be an unforeseen godsend, the representative of a raffle, say, that they'd forgotten they'd entered, or a lawyer's errand boy deliver-ing the will of a recently deceased relative, a cousin that they didn't even know they had.

Usually, it was the woman who opened the door, sur-rounded by any number of squalling children. The husband—

or boyfriend, or lodger, or both—would be sitting at the table in his undershirt, summer or winter.

When I stated the reason for my visit, that I'd come to buy her grandmother's earrings, their wedding bands, his gold-plated *mezuzah,* the women invariably said yes and the men no.

Sometimes, however, an elderly gentleman would answer my knock and invite me in for tea. Only after I'd finished my cup, and eaten the single cracker served on a napkin, would he slip behind the bedroom curtain to discreetly remove his gold bridges, rinse them in the sink (if he had a sink), then reappear and ask, as if as an afterthought, if I wanted to purchase his teeth.

The jeweler for whom I worked didn't care what form the gold came in. He melted down *mezuzahs* and bridges alike. I was supposed to weigh the teeth on a jeweler's scale, but I rarely did. Too often it felt as if I were weighing the worth of the man himself, the very elements from which he was made.

One afternoon, unbeknownst to me, I banged on the door of my first lover, the black-haired boy from the Buttonhole Makers' Union. I didn't recognize him at first. He looked like all the others—wan, indignant, poor. He recognized me, though. I looked, despite my circumstances, anything but poor.

When I asked him if he had gold to sell, he shook his head in bemused impatience, then stared at me unblinking. And then, I did recognize him.

We didn't speak any more this time than we had the last. He pushed me down on his cot as if he was trying to fell me. He kept my arms pinned around his neck. Whatever he was clinging onto, I can only begin to guess. A woman suddenly available and in his bed? A memory? Revenge for my good fortune, though his hands were too kind for revenge, unless kindness itself is a form of reprisal?

I stayed with my union boy until dusk.

Unlike Philip's dalliances, this one never made it into a painting. I have, however, tried to rectify the oversight by offering my buttonhole maker a place on my body, in the form of a sewing needle engraved at the base of my throat. If you look closely, you'll find all my lovers inscribed on my skin.

They started arriving in fits and starts, the refugees from Germany—Albers, Breuer, Grosz—with their incomprehensible accounts of Hitler and his Brownshirts. Philip had known the artists from his days in Berlin, and he insisted on serving as their host by providing them sanctuary until they got their footing on New York's ungiving bedrock. Philip and I hadn't yet lost the refurbished stable on Washington Mews. The landlord hadn't yet had us evicted. But I'm confused. The decade's a little jumbled up. When I picture those early years, it's only Philip and me alone in the house, dreadfully alone, as only poverty can make a couple alone. Perhaps it was just the rumors of fascism that entered our home, and the men were to arrive later. Yes, now I remember, the refugees would arrive later.

Philip retreated further and further into isolation. We rarely went out at night. We couldn't afford to. Mostly, he'd spend his evenings on a folding chair in the studio, a hank of unwashed hair pulled back with one of my old barrettes, a smoldering cigarette hanging from his bottom lip, his overalls a virtual ashtray, all the while not taking his eyes off a blank canvas that had been hanging on the wall for weeks.

One night, to jar him out of his lassitude, I merely asked what he was planning to paint on it. He looked as if I'd distracted him from prayer.

I was at my end of the studio, working on a series of readymades featuring the gold teeth of my customers, the ones I'd filched from the jeweler. At the nadir of the Depression, however, using gold teeth as material, even for shock value, had begun to strike me as a gesture as tactless as Mrs. Whiting's Charity Beggars' Ball.

I walked up behind him, rested my chin on the shelf of his shoulder. I said, "I don't know what I'm doing these days any more than you do, but at least I try."

"Really? What a brave soldier you are." He studied the primed expanse of empty white canvas again. "Is it your art that confuses you? Or could it be our poverty? What are we going to do, Sara?"

"You know I don't care about the money."

"Are you so very sure about that?" He stood up, took my face in his large hands and gently, authoritatively, turned me around, as one might guide a child's gaze to witness an otherwise overlooked spectacle, a burst of fireworks, say, or a rare butterfly. He made me look at my gold-teeth sculptures. "You've never been confused about art a day in your life."

Then he disappeared into our bedroom, tore the sheet off the bed, dragged it back into the studio, and hung it from the ceiling, cleaving the space in two.

For the next few days, the sheet hung between us like the curtain at a Jewish funeral that sequesters the widow or the widower from the rest of the mourners, though, in our case, I'm not quite sure who was grieving for whom.

If the truth be told, Philip was right. We were both in deep and fundamental mourning for the outrageous, arrogant couple we had been, for the cockiness and confidence lost to us when we'd lost Philip's wealth.

Let's just be honest about money and love. Take the defeated, bewildered laborer and his reproachful, silent wife. Take my father and mother. To speak was to argue, so silence prevailed. During Sabbath, after prayers, the rattle of a fork was enough to make you jump. Take the gregarious repartee of Philip's old circle, the bountiful toasts to their good fortune, and the implication that a casual remark might spawn a brand-new reality. At the very least, money provides a couple with something to talk about.

It also provides a couple with a way in which to talk, a self-fulfilled confirmation of their beliefs: we have, therefore we are.

I didn't love Philip for his money, but I did fall in love with the man his money created, and as far as I could glean, that man was disappearing.

I rallied Philip's old comrades, and with their help got him a job assisting Diego Rivera on Rivera's mural *Man at the Crossroads Looking with Hope and High Vision to the Choosing of a New and Better Future.* I believe the upbeat theme was chosen by Nelson Rockefeller himself, patron of the project. At the height of the Depression, Rockefeller had commissioned the mural to adorn his altar to capitalism, Rockefeller Center.

Rivera, though, had a different church in mind. In the center of the wall, he painted Lenin, with his goatee and pointing finger. Behind Lenin's left shoulder, he depicted the United States, symbolized by Wall Street tycoons chugging martinis while mounted police clubbed and bullied unemployed workers. To Lenin's right, he portrayed a Marxist utopia teeming with robust workers cavorting through billowing wheat.

Could Philip and I really have been so naïve as to have been blindsided by the brouhaha the mural caused? The *Times* called Rockefeller Rivera's dupe, his patsy. The Left called Rivera a turncoat, worse than a turncoat, an opportunist, for courting the enemy.

Of course, the mural came down, had to come down. Rockefeller hired the unemployed to chip it off the wall.

We went to the protest. Rockefeller had the plaza barricaded by police mounted on horseback. But even from where we stood, amid the chanting protesters, we could hear chunks of plaster thudding on the floor, see dust wafting out of the building's entrance, enormous puffs of nacreous white dust. And they were standing beside us, the refugees from Germany. Yes, now I remember, an old classmate of Philip's and his sad Jewish wife had arrived the day before. They had come, with their inconceivable accounts of wanton murders, just in time to witness our American tempest in a martini glass.

The glass on my right thigh has been drained of gin and vermouth. The ice cubes have melted. The water has evaporated. All that remains is a gold tooth at the bottom.

CHAPTER FOUR

The accounts the refugees brought with them—rallies of robotic youth, Jews being dragged out of shops and stomped on by children—made no sense to us. Germany was, after all, the birthplace of modern philosophy. What made their accounts particularly horrific, particularly unthinkable, was the age of the perpetrators—rosy-cheeked, stalwart boys. It was as if a farmer from Iowa had appeared at your door, disheveled, dazed, with stories of the Boy Scouts of America rampaging down Main Street, hauling shopkeepers onto the sidewalk and beating them with ax handles.

Most of the refugees stayed with us only a week or so before moving on to prearranged posts—Albers to teach at Black Mountain College, Grosz to the Art Students League. These men were, after all, the crème de la crème of German art. They didn't just add their names to the avant-garde manifestos, as Philip and I had, they wrote them.

With their charming accents, weary demeanors, and encyclopedic educations, they exuded worldliness. If I felt like a shopgirl in their presence, Philip acted like a schoolboy. He deferred to their opinions even when I knew he didn't always agree. He addressed them with exquisite formality. One night, Albers and Grosz asked to see what Philip was working on. I saw him pale. He brought out a few old canvases from his Fauvist-Cubist-Futurist-Dadaist-Surrealist period, then quickly led them past the blank canvas to my side of the studio. While our guests crowded around my tiny teeth sculptures, using a magnifying glass to read the titles that I'd engraved in the gold itself, I watched Philip. By the way he craned his neck forward, the way he smoked his cigarette down to a smudge, I could see how anxious he was that Albers or Grosz or whoever admire my art, acknowledge the exalted value that he himself had placed upon it, and at the same time, I couldn't ignore the suffering in his eyes when he finally realized that his own work, albeit ten years old, was being thoroughly ignored by his old teachers.

Before Albers left for Black Mountain, he introduced us to his New York gallery dealers, Julien and Alice Bronsky, East Side Jews who had been passing as aristocratic Russians for years. As soon as Julien met us, he let us in on their ruse. He let all the artists in on the ruse. A barrel of a man, with eyebrows as white, stiff, and protruding as straw eaves, he used to slap his own rotund cheek when he laughed too hard. Julien and Alice were the last of the Village's avant-garde dealers. They handled the work of Man Ray, Duchamp, de Chirico, Frida Kahlo. Or was it Mina Loy? It hardly matters at this point, now, does it? Everyone is dead but Alice and me.

What mattered was Philip's reaction when the Bronskys offered me, not him, a show. Diplomats of rare sagacity, Julien and Alice spent as much time appraising Philip's work as mine. Alice called Philip's style "eclectic," his decade-old canvases "interesting." Julien said Philip's collection of masks was the most impressive private collection he'd ever seen, a truly remarkable accomplishment. If Philip ever wanted to sell it, he had just the collector. Then he and Alice turned to me and asked, as matter-of-factly as one asks for a glass of water, if I'd be ready to open the fall season. Philip's smile became a frozen shadow of itself, but he managed to kiss me on both cheeks.

"*Mazel tov,*" he whispered.

He retreated into the kitchen for what seemed like a long time. I could hear water splashing, cupboards banging. When he returned, damp hairs clung to his forehead, and he was holding, by the throat, our last bottle of good champagne. He popped the cork, poured out four glasses, proposed a toast to the exhibit's success, then knocked back his drink as if it were wood alcohol.

Late that night, I awoke to the absence of his weight in our bed. The studio light was on. I got up and padded to the doorway.

Philip was back in his folding chair, a freshly rolled cigarette burning in his fist, his hair pulled back with a piece of twine, all the while studying that same expanse of white canvas that had been hanging on the wall for months now. Scattered around his bare feet lay art books, open, faceup, their bright reproductions visible. Philip's gods—Gauguin, Rousseau, Magritte. Now and again, he'd lean forward to stare down at them, as a man gazes into a pond in the hopes of seeing his own reflection.

Philip was bewitched by art. He was so enamored of it that not to contribute to its creation was a betrayal of all he believed. Yet every time he opened his mouth to join in song, a hen's chortle or a donkey's bray came out, and he felt like a mortal punished by his gods.

Had Philip only allowed his art a little ugliness, a little fallibility, a smidgen of human exhaustion. But he didn't. He continued to believe, at forty-three, that art was perfection or it was nothing, and that the avant-garde artist, like the seer, felt only the eternally youthful upsurge of indestructible faith, or he was a fraud. Had Philip just permitted himself a teensy bit of capitulation, he might have realized that every time anyone opens his mouth to join in song, be it Gauguin or Albers, or even me, all we, too, hear is a hen's chortle or a donkey's bray.

I worked for my exhibition with an intensity—no, intensity doesn't convey the magnitude of my ambition. I should say that I worked for this exhibition with an ardor I had never before experienced.

I completed fifty pieces in six months.

And what was Philip doing while I painted? Philip was doing what Philip always did, championing my art, contacting the critics, glad-handing the collectors, sleeping with their wives. He was encouraging me to paint "from the spine," the conduit that connected, in Philip's Surrealist credo, the heart to the mind. He was applauding me so loudly that I finally came to understand that his incessant clapping was in itself a form of punishment.

That fall, 1938, my exhibition opened to—how should I put it?—underwhelming applause? It closed to a barrage of harangues. My comrades on the left labeled me an "esthetic fascist," called my paintings "another example of counterrevolutionary addition: capitalism + hallucinations = surrealism." They went after me with the vitriol of a vicar berating a fallen woman. The conservatives, the Grant Wood realists, dismissed my work as "a hysterical woman's take on the tribulations of marriage."

Am I not the height of old-lady vanity? I can barely recall a line of Shakespeare—

> Her voice was ever something,
> something, and low—an excellent thing in a woman.

—but I can remember every petty slight. Verbatim.

". . . like a knickknack exhumed from your grandmother's attic."

The Bronskys were only able to sell one small piece, and that was to their most ardent collector, John D. Rockefeller, Jr., Nelson's father.

I was devastated. Philip, however, was outraged.

After a snide review in the *Times* had come out, he headed down to the bar where the *Times* critics were said to congregate and got into fisticuffs with my naysayer, a red-faced—red as a Coca-Cola machine—proponent of Americana Regionalist painting.

A week after his bar tussle, still sporting a black eye, Philip was thrown out of the Artists' Union when he commandeered the microphone to rage against its card-carrying membership, who had turned their back on the avant-garde. Before a couple of burly Social Realists dragged him off the stage, he announced that he was going to burn his paintings, cremate his entire oeuvre in a ceremonial conflagration that would illuminate the death of the avant-garde, the only true revolutionary art. He invited everyone to attend. He even challenged those who still maintained a modicum of principle to offer up their own paintings and help stoke the fire.

He borrowed Julien's truck, filled it with his dust-encrusted dreamscapes, his faded utopian cityscapes, and drove to a vacant lot in Hoboken. Beside the rusted remnants of a hobo's camp, he stacked the canvases into an armature for a bonfire. He returned to the truck and carried back his sketchbooks, stuffing them between the paintings. Then he stood back, wiped his face with his coat sleeve, and regarded his life's work, squinting at the heap. His oeuvre barely reached his waist. Tilted this way and that, the paintings looked like a tiny house of cards silhouetted against the late afternoon sun—emblazoned skyscrapers on the other side of the gray Hudson.

There were a dozen of us present—me, Julien, Alice, and the leftover stalwarts of Philip's old bohemia: the ex-Dadaist poet who now wrote, on principle, without ink in the pen; the gray-haired Wobbly who still recounted his one and only talk with Joe Hill; the Futurist painter who refused to believe that Futurism was over.

Philip soaked the tip of a stretcher bar in linseed oil, lit it, and asked me if I wanted to do the honors.

When I wouldn't take his torch, he poured the rest of the oil over the canvases and lit them. At first, his oeuvre just coughed and smoked. Then a blue pillar of fire rose up through the hollow center and exploded into cinders. A couple of seconds later, the flames cascaded over the images. It took less then an hour before everything Philip had ever done was reduced to ash.

Over the next few weeks, I never mentioned his holocaust, not once, and Philip didn't bring up my exhibit, ever.

My own way of stanching the disappointment was to threaten to enlist in the Abraham Lincoln Brigade, to have Philip and me become ambulance drivers for the Spanish

Republic. Aren't avant-garde artists always ambulance drivers in wartime?

"We're not going to Spain," Philip said. "There's nothing for us there, but *tsuris*. Roosevelt and Chamberlain and the rest of the West have no intention of allowing Franco and his fascists to lose. All they really care about is getting rid of the communists. Besides, you can't be an ambulance driver, Sara, because you don't know how to drive."

In the middle of my chest is a palm-sized smudge of ash. It looks like a mistake I tried to blot out, or the mark of the devout, but it's a tattoo like any other. I wanted Philip's sacrificial fire to have a central place in my design.

CHAPTER FIVE

Over the past thirty years, I've given a great deal of thought as to how an urbanite like Philip, a man for whom New Jersey was wilderness, and an East Side Jewess, a woman for whom a canary was wildlife, embarked on the voyage we did take.

Before the Ta'un'uuans begin a journey, they dream their route, then fabricate, to the best of their waking memory, a map of their vision. These maps are three-dimensional spheres of twine and sticks. Into the map's hollow core the islanders place venerated totems of the land that they're leaving—a few grains of sand, a medicinal leaf, a pebble from the altar of their ancestors. No Surrealist doctrine is necessary to convince the Ta'un'uuans that their dream maps are also cages of memory.

Before embarking on our journey, what would Philip and I have placed inside? Ashes from his life's work? A gold tooth from mine? A splinter from our beloved Mews home? Our fathers' *tefillin*? Cages unto themselves, really, holding within their tiny leather cells the words from Exodus reminding every Jew that before he was a wanderer he was a slave.

Right before New Year's, we were awakened by the sound of

hammering on the front door. By the time Philip found his robe and slippers, an eviction notice had been nailed to the jamb. We were given twenty-four hours to pay up all the back rent, or pack up. It wasn't yet dawn. Philip shredded the notice, then raged through the house, while I started to collect what we might salvage. All the furniture—the Breuer chairs, the Le Corbusier chaise longue—had long ago been bartered for either heating oil or art supplies. The Gauguin was gone, offered at auction in '33 for a fraction of its worth. All we had left were the Oceanic masks. I got Philip to stop ranting long enough to help me swathe them in sheets and cart them over to Julien and Alice's.

I reminded them of their promise. I asked them to sell Philip's masks for whatever they could get.

Then I dragged Philip back to the refurbished stable and started sorting through our belongings to see what I could fit into four suitcases, while Philip, wielding a hammer, smashed the Art Deco glass doors, cracked the marble tub. "I'm not leaving that landlord swine anything, Sara, not a shard."

We spent the next few nights on Julien and Alice's sofa, and when we wore out our welcome, at fleabag hotels.

Philip insisted that we sleep fully clothed. "Did you see the bed, Sara? There are pubic hairs on the sheets. Enough to make a wig."

"We'll shake the sheets out," I said.

"That's not the point. The point is they haven't been changed in decades. The point is we don't deserve this."

"No one deserves this," I said.

"Oh, Sara, don't play the little revolutionary with me. You can't take it any more than I can."

He took to sleeping sitting up in a chair. He took to taking long walks by himself. He took to disappearing until midnight. Then one night, he took to not coming back till morning. I lay fully dressed on the pilly blanket and listened to the most unsettling noises coming through the walls—a man hacking, a man praying, a moaning that sounded like a hybrid between human and cat.

The next night, I followed him up to Sutton Place. He entered a townhouse. He had the key. All I could see through the cloudy windows were pinwheels of luminosity from a chandelier.

I banged on the door. Mrs. Blanche "Binky" Whiting IV, all decked out in her new widow's garb, answered my knock.

She folded her arms, studied me, then walked back into the living room. "It's for you, Philip."

Philip had already taken off his coat, had already helped himself to a brandy. He wheeled around and hurried up to me, rubbing my hoarfrosted hands between his. He ushered me inside and closed the door. Helping me off with my coat, he leaned over and whispered, "I'm so happy you're here." And this is the remarkable part: Philip was genuinely happy I had come. "You remember Binky?"

Binky had not aged well. Her face looked pinched. The skin of her throat, once taut, could now be called "liberated." Her gums exploded from her thin lips as she managed a strained smile. She had no choice but to invite me in for a drink.

She said, "By the way, Sara, I saw your show at Julien's," as one lady might say to another, "Your slip is showing."

She took a seat on the living room sofa amid all the comfort and collectibles. Philip selected just the right glass for my brandy, then regaled himself with a sniff of the liqueur. On the

wall over the marble mantle hung an early Ehrenreich, a portrait Philip must have done more than twenty years ago. It
showed a young woman, probably Binky herself, ablaze in Fauvist colors, then fractured into Cubist shards, like something
dropped from a balcony. Evidently, Binky hadn't allowed her
portrait, as I had mine, to be consigned to the flames.

Philip sat down beside her on the sofa and motioned for me
to join them. He patted the cushion next to him, then placed
his hand on my thigh with exquisite lightness. I knew it was
Philip's private way of asking me to spend the night, and I foolishly nodded yes.

It wasn't just that I didn't want to leave him alone with her.
Truth be told, I didn't want to go back to that fleabag hotel any
more than he did.

He whispered something in Binky's ear, and those jack-in-
the-box gums popped out again. She trifled with her diamond
necklace.

Wealth can offset even homeliness. I accompanied them up
the staircase and joined them in bed. Philip and I hadn't "col-
laborated" like this in years. He opted for her bottom half,
while I was left with that mouth, and those tiny breasts, as
yielding to the touch as sodden kitchen sponges.

Binky prattled on the whole time I tried to kiss her. She
gave me explicit directions as to how and where she liked to be
touched, as one gives directions to a lost motorist. Philip was
his usual chivalrous self, graciously divvying up his time between
Binky and me. This was Philip's gift. If attentiveness and inno-
vation eluded him as an artist, they did not elude him as a
lover. There is no other way to put it: Philip *attended* to the
female body.

The instant we were done, though, I couldn't bear the

perfumed scent of her bedsheets, couldn't stand the porcelain figurines that adorned her nightstand. I couldn't suffer the caricatures of our younger selves that Philip and I were calcifying into. I got up and started dressing.

"Where are you going, Sara?" Philip asked.

I picked up my clothes—a shoe, my sweater—and headed out the bedroom door, fully expecting him to trail me at least as far as Binky's foyer, if not all the way back to our hotel, but when I turned to check, I was alone.

Philip returned to our room around nine the next morning. Before he shut the door, before he had a chance to peel off his coat, I had planned to ask him if he was leaving me for her, if he was looking forward to a lifetime of waking up beside her hideous *tchotchkelehs* every morning, but for some reason, it came out, "What the hell do you see in that ugly cunt?"

Philip was silent for a moment. He sat down on the room's only chair and closed his eyes. He stayed like that for so long I actually thought he might have fallen asleep. "She respects me," he said at last.

"Oh, for God's sake, I respect you," I said.

He didn't even bother to open his eyes. "I meant my work, Sara."

"You know I've always admired your work, Philip." I couldn't look at him when I said it, though.

"Then why did you let me burn it?"

"You wanted to burn it."

"Did I?" He tilted his head back against the greasy wallpaper and opened his eyes. "You have no idea what it's like, do you, Sara? On a whim, you decide to become an artist, and sure enough, beauty is waiting at your fingertips. You decide to dabble in the avant-garde, and sure enough, everything you touch turns new." He lifted his head, as one might lift a piece of heavy machinery, and stared at me. "You have no idea what it is to love something, Sara, really, really love it, and not be able to pay it homage. You have no idea how humiliating mediocrity can be."

"That's not true," I said. But I didn't mean it.

I walked over to him and took his face in my hands, fully expecting him to push me away, but he didn't.

"I can't do this much longer. I'm exhausted. I must get away from here."

I didn't know if he was talking about New York, the wretched hotels, or me.

I said, "We can still go to Spain, Philip. Others are going. The Artists' Union sent a contingent last month. At least we'd be a part of something noble—"

"We're not going to Spain."

"We could go out West. To Taos. There are lots of artists there."

"And you'll paint flowers with O'Keeffe until the Depression ends? What will I do? Farm?"

"We could go to Mexico City. The Riveras invited us."

"And wind up in their political battles. No thank you."

"For God's sake, Philip, we could go to Tahiti. Do what Gauguin did."

"Tahiti has been ruined by the French. I've lived with the French, you haven't."

"Then we'll find our own island."

I started to pull my hands away, but he grabbed me by the forearms and kissed my wrists with such a ferocity of tenderness, I would have begged his forgiveness if I'd only known what I'd done.

"Please don't fall in love with somebody else," I whispered.

"I couldn't, even if I wanted to, Sara."

Someone once said that art is arrested attention in the midst of distraction, a definition no less true for the Ta'un'uuans than it is for us. When we stand before a Gauguin or a Goya and experience its beauty, we say, "It took my breath away." For my islanders, to whom breath is the soul, that same moment of rapture is a literal death: art takes their souls away.

The Ta'un'uuan mask is a beacon for the soul. The mask's features are the coordinates for the soul's departure and its return: they serve as a map so that the soul can't lose its way. There are no eye slits, no ear or mouth holes in the Ta'un'uuan mask, only painted facsimiles of eyes and ears and mouths: the dead have no need for the senses; the corporeal world can't reach them any longer, except in song. The artist wakes up the soul in each mask by singing to it.

One week after our "collaboration" with Binky, Julien and Alice sold Philip's mask collection.

Philip, true to form, insisted on being introduced to the collector. When he returned from the meeting, his whole demeanor had changed: he carried himself with his old verve, even going so far as to toss back his hair.

"I've just spent the evening with a man named Richter," he told me, "an industrialist who can buy out the Rockefellers and not even feel it. He calls himself Swiss, but my guess is he's

Bavarian. In any case, he's planning to retire to the Swiss side of Lake Como—'the neutral end,' as he puts it—and build a primitive art museum to end all primitive art museums. He wants my collection in it. He says my Ta'un'uuan masks are the best examples of death masks he's seen outside the Musée de l'Homme. He thinks I have superlative taste. He wants to back me, Sara."

"To curate a mask collection in Switzerland?"

"No, to represent him in the South Seas. He wants me to collect for him."

"Does he know you've never been there? That you bought the masks at a shop in Paris?"

"First of all, it wasn't a shop, it was a vast flea market. And it was packed with junk. Every retired legionnaire was trying to get rid of his African curios, his Tahitian souvenirs. I spent years rifling through those piles of tourist crap until I found my treasures. Collecting requires the same degree of genius that painting does and that's what Richter understands."

"But you don't know anything about that part of the world, Philip."

"I'm not planning on going native. I'm planning on you and me spending a few months of this interminable Depression in the South Seas making money. After all, aren't you the one who wanted to run off and live like Gauguin?"

"Richter's willing to pay for all this?"

"He's willing to pay a generous commission."

"But nothing up front?"

"Just *all* our expenses and two steamship tickets. First-class."

"Isn't Richter a German name? Does he know you're Jewish?"

"What does that have to do with anything? Can't you believe that someone would be willing to back me for once?"

He brushed past me and stood by the window, pushing aside the gray curtain. Our room faced an air shaft: the view was an identical room.

"Just meet him, Sara."

Richter was nothing like the rotund industrialists Rivera had depicted in his mural. He was thin to the point of daintiness and not much taller than I was.

He greeted us himself at the door of his pied-à-terre, a marble mansionette not too far from Binky's. He kissed my bare ring finger with a refinement that bordered on menace and called me "Frau Ehrenreich." He wore a maroon smoking jacket and Moroccan slippers. He offered us champagne, Philip a box of blond cigars. I plucked out one for myself. He said he had a surprise for us. Taking us each by an arm, he led us into his library, a room bricked solid with leather tomes. A steamship brochure lay on his desk, *Pearl of the East.* A giant pink hibiscus bloomed on the cover. A tiny bare-breasted hula girl cavorted on the flower's lengthy pistil.

Richter unfolded the pamphlet. The top half was a map of the South Pacific with a white ocean liner silhouetted in the corner. The ship's route, a red line, zigzagged through the islands—the Friendly Isles, the New Hebrides, the Solomons. The bottom half was a wide-angle photograph of a first-class stateroom, all teak and plush.

"It's a remarkable voyage," Richter said. "I believe the ship crosses the equator three separate times. You see the mark there?" His fingernail tapped on what looked like a printer's error, an ink dot in the middle of nowhere. "That's Ta'un'uu."

Philip and I both leaned closer. Cigar ash spilled onto the brochure. Philip carefully brushed it off.

"It's a Japanese shipping line, a merchant vessel," Richter explained, "but as you can see, no expense is spared for the lucky few passengers who tour with it. The Japanese are extraordinary hosts, and of late, they've become rather enchanted by the South Seas. The ship is calling at every major port, and where it's not officially calling, arrangements can be made. For a collector like Philip it's the chance of a lifetime." He slipped the brochure into Philip's breast pocket, then replenished our champagne flutes. "When you finally get to Tokyo, if you'd both like, you can return by land. The Trans-Siberian sleeping cars are said to be from the tzar's time, true Victorian carriages. We can rendezvous at Lake Como."

"If war doesn't break out in Europe first," I said.

"All the more reason to be off in the South Seas," Philip said.

"You don't think the pact between the tyrant and the thug will hold, Frau Ehrenreich?"

I asked him who was who.

"Why, Stalin is the tyrant. Adolf is only a thug. Do you know how I know?"

I said I didn't.

"The size of their mustaches."

He motioned for us to follow him into a high-domed chamber off the library. Its walls were bare and pocked with nail holes. "I must apologize. My treasures were put in storage yesterday. It takes so much preparation for them to be shipped home. I'm sorry you didn't get to say goodbye to your masks, Philip. All I have left is my private collection. Would you like to see that?"

He opened another door to yet another domed room. On every surface—the antique tables, the rosewood bookcases, the marble pedestals—carved figurines copulated, or mated with animal deities, or squatted licentiously.

He picked one up and set it on the platter of his palm—a six-inch-high fur-and-shell-ornamented female icon divulging her sexual organs, a mother-of-pearl shell. "She's from the Trobriands, one of the islands the ship will be calling at. Sexuality in the Trobriands is said to be reversed: women are the aggressors. During the yam harvest, marauding bands of girls have been known to rape a man."

Philip laughed and asked how that was possible.

"You'll have to tell me when you get back," Richter said, steering us toward a shelf on which a bone-white tusk coiled upward. "It's from the New Hebrides. It's a pig's tusk. Can you make out the markings?"

Etched lightly into the ivory, hundreds of creatures with two sets of genitalia, male and female, coupled in bewildering possibilities.

"On Ambae, where the tusk is from, raising swine is considered an art form. The islanders have somehow managed to breed a rare hermaphrodite pig. They regard its ivory as divine because it has the power of both sexes."

He opened a glass cabinet and lifted out a wooden box. "We should put out our cigars. This is very old and fragile." He peeled off the lid. A shrunken head sat nestled in cotton batting. Faded tattoos covered every square inch of its rigid face—a turtle with human hands, wings instead of eyebrows, a shark on one cheek, an albatross on the other.

"Tattoos were once believed by the Ta'un'uuans to be scars that can sing."

I must have been gaping.

"Don't worry, Frau Ehrenreich. It's from the early eighteen hundreds. The Ta'un'uuans are all good Christians now. Methodists, I believe. I'm hoping that Philip will be able to find me a few more of those extraordinary masks." He turned the head slightly, so that we could inspect the shriveled, marked ears. "See how the tattooing has inspired the mask designs?"

He put the head back into the box, then rang a little bell. A side door opened and a thick-necked butler wheeled in a three-dimensional model of his museum, a cardboard Roman edifice cantilevered over a lake. It looked like something Speer might design.

"It's quite regal, don't you think?" He tapped on a paper cupola. "I'm reserving that wing for your finds, Philip." He looked at me, Philip, me again. "That is, if you permit him to go, Frau Ehrenreich."

He lifted off the roof so we could see the columned interior.

I wanted to tell him he needn't bother with the hard sell any longer. Between the art he'd just shown us, the champagne, and the photo of the stateroom, I was half-packed already. The deal was truly sealed for me, however, the moment Richter had called it Philip's wing.

So what venerated totems did we finally pack into our cages of memory? With Richter footing the bill, Philip packed three new linen suits, one gabardine one, three pairs of hand-sewn Italian shoes, a tuxedo, a dozen French shirts and the gold cuff links to go with them, and silk pajamas and a silk bathrobe. For traipsing around the islands, he purchased three bright orange sarongs and two pairs of leather sandals: "I'm not walking among them like a colonial." For where no hotel accommodations were available, he bought a watertight pup tent, two air mattresses, three hurricane lamps, and a portable canvas bathtub.

For my ship wardrobe, I shopped at Macy's. I couldn't be bothered wasting my time purchasing clothes. My vices included French oil paints, Belgian linen, and Winsor & Newton brushes. Richter even tantalized me with a Japanese folding easel that popped open like an umbrella for landscape painting.

For barter with the island carvers, we acquired five cases of axes and knives. To pay tribute to their chiefs, we purchased fifty cigarette lighters and ten kilos of pipe tobacco. To entrance their wives, we bought a box of rhinestone jewelry on Orchard Street, the kind my mother had loved to wear.

Were our presents demeaning? Perhaps. But any more so than the trinkets with which Richter had just enticed us?

The ship tattooed on my back is not the one we sailed on. *Pearl of the East* was as grand and elegant as Richter had promised, whereas the vessel on my back is anything but elegant. It's an old rusty freighter, and its hull spans the whole of my shoulders.

It's one of my earliest designs. I chose the shoulder blades because I thought the bone there would make the procedure less painful. It's only beginner's luck that the cargo ship is tattooed exactly where it should be, that I carry its burden on my back.

PART TWO

GAN EDEN

CHAPTER SIX

In the beginning, there was only God's breath, which became the first song. God then sang into existence the sun, and the stars, which are but musical notes suspended in the night sky; and all the oceans, and the ocean's currents, which are but melodies moving through liquid.

In the center of his chorale, the islanders believe, God created Ta'un'uu, the Garden of Eden, and peopled it with Adam, whom he made from ash, and Eve, whom he made from coral. God then breathed into his creations the gift of song and completed their paradise by giving them cargo: tinned meat, steel tools, rice in bags, tobacco in tins, and matches, but not cotton clothing.

Adam and Eve were content for a while, but eventually they offended God by improving upon his design. They beautified their naked bodies with drawings of the turtle, the cockatoo, the sago palm, the tobacco tins, and the wooden matchsticks. Beguiled by their own splendor, they copulated against God's commandment that they remain chaste. In his fury, God created rain to erase their drawings and threw them out of Paradise to wander the bush. He took away their cargo and decreed that they should spend the rest of their days living on the barest necessities.

Later, Adam accidentally tore his tongue on a charred piece of fish bone and discovered the art of indelible tattooing (to penetrate the flesh with ash, to affix it to the soul with pain), a technique he taught to his sons, Cain and Abel. When Cain slew Abel, it was because Abel's tattoos so diminished his own creations. This act of artistic murderous jealousy set the seal on man's wickedness, and the fall of man was complete.

The situation continued until the time of Noah. Noah was a good man who obeyed God and taught his sons to do likewise. All the other human beings on earth were still mired in depravity, arousing their lust with tattoos, and copulating, so God decided to destroy them in a great flood. He gave Noah a cargo ship, which contained tinned meat and rice in bags, and matches, and fitted Noah with a peaked cap, white shirt, shorts, and shoes, and told Noah to save his family and all the animals, which Noah did. Then God sent a typhoon that lasted for forty days and forty nights.

When the water subsided, God instructed Noah to repopulate the world and to relish the cargo. God explained to Noah that the cargo was His reward for Noah's devotion. Everything was good for a while until Noah's son, Ham, disobeyed God's will. He espied his father's nakedness, which he found appalling in its starkness, and cut into his own flesh with a burnt fish bone. In his agony, Ham muttered God's name in vain.

God was again very angry, and he took away the cargo and banished all of Noah's sons to different places on the earth. Because Noah was a good man and these were his sons, God offered them a reprise in the form of a choice. They could either go into the bush with a bow and arrow or with a rifle. The bow and arrow was lighter than the metal stick, so the most pragmatic of Noah's sons chose the bow and arrow. His descendants became the Ta'un'uuans. The other sons chose the rifles and their descendants became the white man.

The Ta'un'uuans worked very hard, and with the help of missionaries, eventually found their way back to God. They gave up tattooing and nakedness. But God continued to punish them, for no good reason, with diseases and blights and typhoons. He withheld the cargo even though they obeyed the missionaries and destroyed the skull masks of their ancestors. Then God in his wisdom realized his mistake and sent his only child, Jesus, down from heaven to earth to make amends with the Ta'un'uuans and compensate them for their unjust suffering.

Jesus was both a black man and a white man, who could transfigure himself into animals and who spoke all the languages on earth.

Jesus told the Ta'un'uuans that he had suffered on the cross as they had suffered under the tattoo needle. He told them to disobey the missionaries and again initiate their bodies through pain, again make skull masks and sing to the masks so that their ancestors would hear them.

Jesus said their ancestors were safe with his father in heaven, which had chairs, tables, and beds, and meals of tinned meat cooked and served by angels, and whiskey for all. Jesus said if they obeyed him, their ancestors would send the cargo, which would arrive by freighter.

Jesus then turned himself into a turtle with human hands and swam off.

CHAPTER SEVEN

What could they have made of us?

Philip stood braced at the skiff's prow, his Buffalo Bill hair flying, his orange sarong slapping against his blond legs, a sandaled foot up on the gunwale; I was huddled in the bottom of the rolling boat, trying to keep from being ill.

Ta'un'uu, a vertical green eruption garlanded with pink sand and white surf, was about a half mile away.

It was our first stop in the South Seas. We were the only passengers disembarking. The island was too nominal a destination to rate an official port of call, the harbor too shallow an anchorage to accommodate the *Pearl of the East.* Captain Hirata had agreed to shuttle us ashore by dinghy, and pick us up in ten days' time on his return voyage from Tarawa.

In the Ta'un'uuans' cosmology, only what has already been sung into existence is perceivable. In their musical arrangement of space and time, the past is before us, and the future behind. The soul must face his ancestors, while the body steps backward into the unknown.

Philip and I were only as real to them as the refrains we evoked in their ancestors' songs.

Accordingly, Philip might have been a seventeenth-century sandalwood trader, or an eighteenth-century slaver, or a modern missionary. With his shoulder-length hair and orange "skirt," he might even have been a missionary's big blond wife. And me, in my equally inappropriate attire? A boy's linen suit bought off a sale rack at Macy's, a Panama hat fastened around my chin with Philip's shoelaces. Perhaps I was a white ghost modeling the cotton clothes that will one day arrive by cargo ship?

There were about two hundred of them standing on the beach, small-boned people with burnt sienna skin and elaborate hairdos. The men wore foot-long penis gourds, the women straw skirts, the children nothing. Our steamship's engines must have awakened them at dawn; its enormous hull must have blotted out their sunrise.

Our arrogance must have astonished them.

We didn't ask permission to enter their fishing waters and land a skiff. We didn't acknowledge their chief before sloshing onto their beach and wringing out our sodden pant cuffs and sarong.

The two sailors who had motored us ashore started tossing our gear up onto the beach, and we didn't so much as stop them and face our hosts and ask if these intrusions were wanted, let alone bearable. We were like houseguests who not only show up uninvited but also arrive with mounds of luggage for an indefinite stay: air mattresses, pup tent, Primus stove, hurricane lamps, portable tub, folding easel, and steamer trunks filled with axes and costume jewelry.

The islanders should have done to us what their ancestors did to castaways and beachcombers—club us unconscious, cut us into small pieces, and boil us with sweet potatoes. Instead, they watched with mounting amazement as the two sailors pushed off in the skiff, leaving them with the enormous blond hermaphrodite and his cotton-clad ghost companion. Decorously, they averted their eyes from ours: to stare was to be the aggressor.

But we stared. We'd just spotted their tattoos—a turtle with human hands, stick figures in coitus, in prayer, in battle, an ark, a cockatoo, a praying mantis, a bolt of lightning, and abstractions that looked as if ants had been dipped in ink and let loose upon the body.

The colors were indigo, cinnabar, viridian, and lampblack. No body part was exempt—not earlobes or throats or fingers or toes, not even lips.

The islanders stood shoulder-to-shoulder on the pink sand. When one of them shifted a foot, or turned his head, or twisted in any way, the effect was that of a great tapestry billowing.

I tried to catch Philip's eye, but he was already moving toward them. He had to hoist up the wet hem of his sarong so that he could walk without tripping.

The women burst into a salvo of giggles.

Philip laughed at himself, too, a little too exuberantly. "I was told you speak English," he said, smiling. But I could hear the tremor in his voice. Philip wasn't frightened of these people. He was never frightened of the alien, the strange, the beautiful. No, Philip was terrified that if he didn't succeed here, while there might be other islands, other opportunities for collecting, this particular failure would leech away his confidence, and then it wouldn't matter where we went.

Not a soul responded.

He steeled himself and marshaled on. "Thank you for allowing us to visit your beautiful island. My name is Philip, and this is my wife Sara. We have come a very long way because your mask makers are great, great artists, and we believe the world should know this and honor you because of it. We are artists ourselves, and if you will allow us, we would be grateful to witness your master carvers at work and to offer them, and you and your chiefs, gifts in exchange for their creations. Sara, why don't you show them our gifts."

I opened the steamer trunk and held up a steel ax and a string of plastic pearls. I would have offered them the cotton clothes off my back if they would only trade their masks with him.

No one said anything. They didn't even whisper among themselves.

Finally, an old woman broke ranks and stepped forward. By her regal manner, she was obviously of high rank. Her hair was teased into a voluminous cone and adorned with seashells. Her face was tattooed from ear to ear: I couldn't quite read her expression. Threatening? Curious? Walking right up to us, she folded her arms over her large flat breasts and studied Philip, me, the ax, the gaudy necklace, our gear, then Philip again. She had to crane her neck skyward to meet his eye: she was shorter than I was. Finally, she turned her back on us and walked away, motioning the others to follow.

Some of the younger men and women wanted to come over and see what else was in our trunk, but they obeyed the old woman, dispersing into the forest. It was like watching a great tapestry being torn apart and the tatters coming to life.

. . .

The islanders had designed themselves so that the sum of their creation was always greater than its parts. An individual's tattoos were considered by the tribe to be no more meaningful than a word taken out of context.

This is why, when viewed singularly, as I am viewed these days, my tattoos don't seem nearly as profound as I claim them to be. To the squeamish who can't quite bear to look at me, I'm a mere curiosity; to those who do look, really look, I must seem the most isolated of souls.

CHAPTER EIGHT

Philip started heaving our provisions away from the oncoming tide before everything got soaked and ruined, while I sat down uselessly in the sand. I'd been given hints of grandeur in the past—the New York skyline at sunset, pinwheels of luminosity cast by a chandelier—but nothing had prepared me for this. We were in the bowl of a vast natural amphitheater. The mountains ascended around us in ancient, dripping green terraces. Their pinnacles were viridescent. Vapors wafted out of the foliage. Clouds were born on the cliffs. Everywhere, lace-thin waterfalls plunged into their own rainbows.

I was by the water's edge. The sand was the consistency of talcum powder. A red bird, sporting a sapphire crown as elaborate as a French wig, landed on a conch shell by my foot. Two periscope eyes popped out from the shell's hole. The sea was azure in the shallows, red-violet over the sea grass, milky blue in the sandbars. Where the orange and purple reef touched the open sea, cobalt swells exploded into white mist.

I simply assumed that all this beauty had inspired the tattoos.

Isn't that the epitome of arrogance? Five minutes in the company of nature's rapture, and I presumed I understood.

I looked around at Philip, who was hauling the last of our trunks away from the surf.

"Do you think they're coming back to eat us?" I asked.

"They're Christians. Methodists."

"Tattooed Methodists?"

He came over and collapsed beside me on the sand. His face and chest were dripping. He used the hem of his sarong to mop them up. For a couple of minutes, we just gawked at all this splendor. Then Philip turned and stared at the jungle.

"They were living art, weren't they, Sara?"

I wanted to pitch our tent by the sheltered rocks, but Philip insisted we make camp on the beach, fully exposed to the wind and the sun. When I questioned his judgment, he said we needed to be where the villagers could see us at all times, so that they might learn to trust us. Philip unpacked the tent while I tried to make sense of the instructions that came with it. Now and again, we could hear the village dogs barking just within the thicket of jungle, but when I turned to look, all I could see was a blockade of greenery.

I had slept outdoors only once before in my life, at a Zionist camp in the Catskills. I had kept as close to the fire as possible without incinerating myself and joined my sweet young comrades in songs about how our people would one day return to the merciless wilderness and transform it into an Eden.

Philip and I lit a fire. All the books had said to light a fire.

It was ninety degrees under the palms.

We opened a can of peaches and a tin of mackerel for supper. We ate in silent edginess, alert to every cracking branch and hooting creature. Now and then, voices or a high note of laughter was borne on the wind, but we couldn't gauge how far the sounds had traveled.

The light began tapering. A fan of mauve opened on a dissolving horizon. Silver-tooled clouds hung motionless in pink and gold space. The sun slipped behind a scaffolding of burnt-scarlet vapor, then plunged into the gilded sea. The planets came out one by one in the blue-violet sky. Then, without transition, the fabric of the night was dusted with stars.

"Das es Gan Eden?" I asked Philip in Yiddish.

But Philip was asleep.

The next morning, Philip ornamented a dwarf palm near camp with a glinting display of axes and jewelry. He twirled one of the dangling pendants so that its cut glass caught the morning light and spun in its own prism.

"Has anyone been here?" I asked, crawling free of the tent's flaps.

Philip looked up from the mesmerizing shimmer. His face was dripping, and it wasn't even eight in the morning. "Should I put out more axes? I need to hold something back to bargain with later. What do you think of the display? Do you think it's too much?"

I foolishly said, "It's as enticing as a Macy's spring sale."

He didn't ask my opinion again.

He opened his knapsack and took out an oversize art book, flipping through the pages until he found what he was looking for. He walked back to the dwarf palm and angled the open tome against the trunk, amid the axes. Page right showed Picasso's *Les Demoiselles d'Avignon,* page left an array of Oceanic and African masks from which the ladies' visages had been so obviously inspired.

Blotting up his brow with the crook of his damp arm, he sat down a few feet away from me and opened two warm beers and a tin of biscuits for breakfast.

"I think the Picasso's a brilliant touch. I'm not just saying that," I said.

He ate without taking his eyes off the dwarf palm.

Not a soul came.

The sun went up and down in the cloudless sky. The rollers, pounding against the distant reef, were marbled with orange phosphorescence. The only light was a flaring green disk on the vanishing horizon. After dusk, when the mosquitoes came out, I crawled back into the tent and shrouded myself in netting, but Philip just batted away the bugs and stood by the blackening sea. Finally, it became too dark to see my own hand. I couldn't find the flashlight. I shut my eyes and tried to will myself to sleep. Sometime before I dozed off, I heard the tent flap open, felt the brush of netting as Philip crawled inside. He lay down by my side. Sweat pooled where our skin touched. "Please pray this works, Sara."

On the second morning, our only visitors were crabs and gulls. Just as panic began to set in, just as Philip and I finished our twentieth cigarette of the morning when we'd rationed ourselves two, an old man—sixty? seventy? one hundred?—walked into our camp trailed by a young woman in a shaggy straw skirt. Her bare breasts were so huge and projectile, they came at us like hurled footballs. The old man wore only a carapace of tattoos and an ornamented string around his waist, tied to his foreskin, pulling his penis upright.

Philip and I were under the tent's canopy, sorting through our provisions for breakfast.

The old man ambled over and squatted between us. He placed his hand on Philip's chest, then insisted that Philip do likewise. When he was sure that Philip had felt his heart beat, he gestured to the bright gold Del Monte can in Philip's other hand. The label showed a halved peach as idyllically rendered as any vegetation engraved on the old man's skin.

Philip pantomimed eating from the can with his fingers, then reached for his camp knife, punctured the seal, sawed open the lid, and placed the tin in the tattooed hands.

The old man examined the peaches drowning in the thick gold syrup. He lifted the can, sniffed it, fished out a wedge, closed his eyes (even his eyelids were tattooed) and bit into it. A moment later, he shook his head in wonder.

"This exceptional, most exceptional," he said.

"It's called a cling peach in heavy syrup," Philip explained. "Would you like to try a different fruit?"

"Yes, please."

Philip opened a can of pears and set them in front of our guest.

Dipping his hand into the syrup (even the webbing between his fingers was tattooed), the old man plucked out a slice, tilted back his head, and lowered the milky green sliver into his mouth (even the underside of his throat was tattooed). Again, he was taken aback by delight.

"Equally exceptional."

"Your English is very good," I said.

"I was a Christian schoolboy, sir."

The Ta'un'uuan pronunciation of English is impossible to replicate. Pages would be overrun with hyphens and apostrophes, yet they would no more reproduce the old man's inflections than when my own East Side accent has been reduced to "Waddayuh wan?" The islanders hold words in their throats for as long as they can before allowing each syllable to issue forth in piping highs and crackling lows, like the last throes of a gospel hymn played on a scratchy gramophone.

The young woman stood a few feet behind us, head lowered, breasts up, watching everything from an oblique angle. Philip motioned for her to join us, but she covered her face with her hands and wouldn't budge.

She mumbled something into her palms.

The old man translated, "My daughter's daughter very much curious: 'What island you belong?' "

"The island of Manhattan," Philip said, turning to face the young woman.

She lowered her hands slightly, revealing a canny, infectious, nervy gaze, and emitted another sequence of muffled breaths.

"My daughter's daughter very much curious: 'What dances belong on the island of Manhattan?' "

For a moment, Philip looked as puzzled as he was charmed. He rose to his feet, rehitched his sarong, and bowed rakishly to the young lady. "Would you care to dance?"

The girl shyly looked down.

He offered her his hand. "Men and women always dance together on the island of Manhattan," he explained.

The girl's eyes lifted in marvel, but she shook her head no.

I got to my feet and snatched the hand.

"Philip," I said.

"Sara," he said.

He jerked me to his chest, clasped the small of my back in one hand, my wrist in the other, and wielded me across the sand in a tango.

The old man watched in drop-jawed surprise, then exploded into giggles, which he politely tried to stifle by slapping his hand over his mouth.

Quickening our pace, Philip and I segued into the Lindy, the Charleston, then something vaguely resembling Isadora Duncan's gazelle leaps, before collapsing on the sand, parched and panting.

The old man, having given up trying to suppress his shrieks of laughter, began whistling and clapping in what is evidently the universal display of jubilation.

His granddaughter stood silently behind him, watching Philip with brazen inquisitiveness, though her hands continued to veil her face. She leaned over and whispered to her grandfather in their breathy language, letting out a slow exhalation of steady puffs, the sounds I make, to my own ears at least, when blowing smoke rings.

"My daughter's daughter say she must hear 'what songs belong on the island of Manhattan.'"

Philip smiled at the girl and said, "Give me a second to catch my breath." He wiped away the sweat stinging his eyes, then rose to his feet and faced his audience. He took on the inflated, heroic stance of an Irish tenor.

The pose alone was enough to make the old man applaud.

Philip cleared his throat and sang:

Arise, you prisoners of starvation!
Arise, you criminals of want.
For justice thunders condemnation.
A better world's in birth.
No more tradition's chains shall bind us.
Arise, you slaves, no more in thrall!
The earth shall rise on new foundations.
We have been naught, we shall be all.
'Tis the final conflict:
Let each stand in his place.
The international working class
Shall be the human race.

Philip took a full bow.

The old man brought his hands together in a single, ear-splitting clap. His black eyes, two wet stones, gleamed at Philip through the thicket of his facial tattoos. "Was your song a prayer?" he asked at last.

"In a manner of speaking," Philip said. "It's a prayer for some of us."

"On the island of Manhattan?"

"Yes. And other places. Many, many other places."

The girl blew into her grandfather's ear.

"My daughter's daughter say she very much want to sing for you now."

The girl let her hands slide down her face. A tiny, unfinished tattoo, her only one, flowered on the pink ledge of her bottom lip. She threw back her head, Al Jolson–style, and let loose a deep, rattling, unbroken wail. The song was plainly reverent, that much I could tell, though it hardly resembled an ethereal Christian hymn or an earthy cantor's cry. Her song sounded subterranean, cavernous, as if the island were hollow, and all its gases, the very air that allowed it to stay afloat, were escaping through her lips.

The old man stood and walked over to the shady spot where Philip had sung. Spreading out his thin arms, eagle-fashion, then drawing up one bony leg, flamingo-style, he struck a pose. He remained balanced on one leg, without so much as swaying, for as long as it took his granddaughter to empty her lungs.

Then he began to dance, though dance doesn't exactly define it: he choreographed his tattoos. He flexed his pectorals and a shark lurched. He tensed his shoulder and a tuna jumped. He hardened his biceps and a blowfish puffed up. He tightened his other arm and a stick figure grew pregnant. He worked the muscles in his abdomen, buttocks, and thighs until all the creatures on his flesh either pounced or bolted.

When he'd run through his menagerie, he struck another pose, hunched over and reptilian. He held it until his granddaughter finished singing. Then he opened his mouth, as wide as it would go, and slowly unfurled his tongue.

The tip was as grooved and inked as a totem pole.

Philip clapped to beat the band, but I winced, then looked away.

The old man saw me wince and look away. I gave a Bronx whistle and started applauding, but it was too late. When I next caught his eye, there was a baffled, hurt cast in his gaze.

Of course, now my own tongue is tattooed. It's the last procedure I had done to me before *Life* "discovered" me. My grand finale, perhaps even my masterpiece, though what can "master-piece" mean when the work of art is anything but immortal? Besides, don't all old artists need to believe that their final work is their finest hour?

A tattoo on the tongue is extremely rare and prestigious. It is customarily reserved for the very old and the very devout. It requires a herculean effort on the part of both the artist and his human subject. The tongue's texture alone makes the work blindingly exacting, and since the organ itself is but a clump of nerves, engraving it is a form of slow torture.

In the Ta'un'uuan language, the word "tongue" is as weighted with meaning as the word "heart" is in English. A tongue can lust, ache, break. One can be "heavy-tongued," "hard-tongued," or "tongue-sick." One can even make love with "half a tongue."

When you examine mine, you'll find no identifiable icons, no cargo ships, or death masks of Philip; just a galaxy of specks. Had I engraved a recognizable image on my tongue, it would have been an act of betrayal to the islanders: they believe an image on the tongue alters the truth of every word one speaks. The tongue, after all, is what shapes the song.

CHAPTER NINE

The old man told us his name. It sounded, to my ears, like
a measure of music played backward. When Philip tried
to pronounce it, it came out as gibberish a madman might
utter. The old man finally suggested we call him by his boy-
hood Christian name, Ishmael, and we call his granddaughter,
Ishmael's daughter's daughter.

Philip offered our guests another round of canned fruit,
then sat down across from Ishmael and asked if he knew any
master carvers who might be willing to sell us their creations.
Philip might as well have asked him if he knew where we could
buy yesterday's sunset.

Ishmael's brows, a pair of tattooed wings, rose as if to take
flight.

Philip put it a different way. Did Ishmael know any carvers who wanted a new ax in exchange for a mask that was no
longer of value?

Ishmael turned his eyes to Philip's display. The palm was
ripe with steel and glass fruit. The art book leaned against the
trunk. Ignoring the pendants and hatchets, Ishmael picked up
the book, glanced at the naked mademoiselles from Avignon,
then closely, painstakingly examined the reproduction of his

ancestors' skull masks. He held the page inches from his face. He grazed his finger lightly over the illusion, then quickly flipped the page over to see if he could find the masks' back sides. An altogether different sculpture, Brancusi's *Bird in Flight,* greeted him. He shook his head in wonder and bewilderment, then carefully set the book down—facedown—and began perusing our camp, trailed by his granddaughter. Whispering among themselves, they took in our waterproof tent, our air mattresses, our canvas bathtub, our coffeepot, and our stockpiles of tinned provisions, enough to feed a brigade for a month.

"What purpose do my masks serve you?" he finally asked.

"We're going to take them across the ocean, two oceans," Philip added.

"*Two* oceans?"

"Yes, to a museum, a grand house where our people gather to worship beauty. Your carvers' masks will have an honored place in this house, a room of their own, and their names will be written on the wall beside their creations. If you have carvings to trade, Ishmael, your name will be written there, too, so that the whole world will know who you are."

Ishmael seemed beguiled by the concept, though I couldn't tell if his enchantment was due to his chance for fame or because he'd just been informed there was another ocean in the world.

Hunkering down again, he told Philip that he was a master carver himself, that he worked not just on wood and yams, but on human bodies. He motioned for his granddaughter to sit beside him, then gently pulled down her lower lip to reveal for us the full mastery of his skills: the tattoo, a Kandinsky abstraction, extended all the way down to her pink gums. He said he had masks and spirit poles for trade, but, "most unfortunately," he already owned three metal axes, he had no use for more, and his wives preferred shell necklaces over glass ones.

He started to rise, as did his granddaughter, in a badly staged pantomime of leaving.

"Ishmael," Philip said, "I find it hard to believe that you and your granddaughter see nothing whatsoever in our entire camp that you don't want or need."

The old man settled down again and rattled off, like a housewife ticking off a grocery list, precisely what he and his granddaughter wanted: three cans of cling peaches, three jars of apricots, six tins of mackerel, the box of matches sitting on our stovetop, and the twenty sticks of tobacco jutting out of Philip's shirt pocket.

Philip handed over our pack of Chesterfields.

"We need also the cotton clothes when you leave," Ishmael added. He fitted the cigarettes painstakingly under his string belt so that the twine didn't tug too much on his tethered penis, then motioned for Philip and me to follow him and his granddaughter into the jungle.

Everything was oversized, sticky, swarming. The ground was freakishly alive. Every footfall crushed something mortal. Up close, the palm trunks were as hairy as apes. Prickly vines coiled around every root, strangled every sapling. Red lichen bloomed on the wet stones. Beetles as big as dessert plates scurried by. Above, in the undulating canopy, cockatoos honked, trilled, whistled, and shrieked.

Now and then, I could see a cluster of huts, haystacks on stilts, in an open field of grass.

Ishmael steered us away from the village and toward a swamp thick with vermilion butterflies. The insects alighted on our brows and backs, lips and throats, greedily siphoning up our perspiration through their hollow proboscises.

The swamp smelled like boiled eggs and was the color of motor oil. In the middle of its black surface, floating among the sago stumps, was a tree-trunk carving, a life-sized male figure, attached to the shoulders of a life-sized female figure, who in turn became a canoe prow. The canoe was captained by a wooden praying mantis, or a human praying; I couldn't tell which.

Both figures were roughly chiseled except for their genitalia, which were impeccably crafted and painted red. Ishmael had accorded these organs the same attention to detail that, say, Vermeer gave the human face.

"Is this the carving you want us to have?" Philip asked. He was trying to contain his excitement: the piece was exquisite.

"Yes," Ishmael said. He picked up a branch and pushed aside the algae clogging the bank to reveal a whole watery cemetery of masks and figurines half-buried in the silt.

"Are *all* these for trade?"

"Yes," Ishmael said.

"May I go and pick a few out?"

"Yes."

Philip gathered up his sarong, then gingerly waded up to his thighs in the bog.

"Just watch out for snakes," I said.

Keeping his chin well above the black water, Philip knelt

down and blindly groped for whatever he could reach. He dragged out four masks and a tiny wooden couple locked in coitus. He peeled off his wet shirt, then lay the pieces out in the sunlight to dry. Their wood was sodden, but not to the point of rot: the pieces must have been sealed with resin.

"Which is your favorite, Ishmael?" I asked. "Which carving do *you* like best?"

Ishmael squatted down to survey his old pieces—the boar mask with spiral tusks, the one with a steel nail coiffure, the "early Picasso." He touched each one as lightly as you would the cheek of someone sleeping. Finally, he smiled and pointed to the carving still adrift in the swamp.

"It would have been my choice, too," Philip said.

"And which carving do you like least?" I asked.

Ishmael's smile imploded: either he didn't understand my question, or else he understood it only too well.

"Ishmael," I pressed on, "which one do you think is less"— I groped for the mot juste—"worthy than the others?"

Ishmael knelt over his carvings and cupped his ear against their wood. He wore the same expression of clinical concentration that a doctor does when listening for a heartbeat. When he finally finished with the last one, he looked up at me, stricken. "Must I say?" he asked.

"Certainly not," Philip said, shooting me a look of contempt, though I knew that he, too, couldn't tell if Ishmael's performance was authentic or part of the negotiations.

Of course, had I been a little less suspicious and a little more observant, I would have seen that by taking the pulse of the wood, Ishmael was only trying to ascertain from his art what I have tried to ascertain from mine: is there any life inside?

A raindrop as solid as a marble struck my shoulder, then another crashed on Ishmael's head. We both looked up. The sun was still out, but the thrum of rain was advancing across the treetops. Ishmael's granddaughter picked up a fallen palm frond and quickly held it up above her grandfather's head, while Philip and I dashed for the canopy.

Moments later, water began pouring through the leaves and branches.

Ishmael drew his shivering granddaughter under the leaf umbrella, and without so much as a word or a wave goodbye to us, they started hurrying down the path toward their village.

"Ishmael," Philip shouted after him, "are you coming back to camp later?"

"Yes, and my daughter's daughter will come pick up our cling peaches."

CHAPTER TEN

We waited inside the pup tent all afternoon for Ishmael and his granddaughter to return, but the storm only grew more fierce. Around three, Philip made a dash for the swamp anyhow, and hauled back two of the masks. Blotting them off with our only blanket, he examined them in the beam of his flashlight. "These are his discards, Sara, what he tossed in the swamp. My God, either one of them will justify Richter's investment in me. Don't you think?"

By nightfall, it was blowing and raining with the force of a fire hose. I couldn't tell if we were in any danger, or if this was just a typical squall in the South Seas. For New Yorkers like ourselves, weather had always been an abstraction: a storm was a spectacle witnessed through window glass; rain was what you experienced while folding your umbrella to duck into a taxi.

All I knew about being caught in a gale was a couple of edicts recollected from my Zionist camp days: *Do not touch your tent's skin, or it will commence leaking. Do not wear your steel wristwatch; steel attracts lightning.*

Philip and I lay huddled together in the center of the tent, our wrists bare, listening with mounting panic to the pandemonium outside. Coconuts crashed all around us. Waves pummeled the shore. Thunder rolled across the water. Palms creaked and banged. And always, always, there was the wind, as shrill and deafening as the el train hurtling overhead.

Suddenly, a corner of our tent tore loose and began snapping violently back and forth. Philip tried to grab hold of it, but the wind was too strong.

Then, one by one, the grommets ripped open, and the cables came loose. They began flogging the canvas. Next, the poles pulled free of the wet sand, and the pegs gave way. During one particularly fearsome gust, the whole tarpaulin popped open like a sail and took off into the night sky, pulling the poles with it. The pegs hurled back and forth on the snapping cables, like a cat-o'-nine-tails.

Philip and I remained supine on the air mattresses, the rain pelting our faces: we were crystallized in shock. The sensation was somewhere between losing your umbrella to a sudden gust and losing your roof to a tornado.

Philip raised his head to assess our damage, but the blowing sand forced his eyes shut.

"We have to get off this beach, we have to find shelter," he shouted. He rolled over and pushed himself up against the hurling debris, shielding his eyes with one hand while helping me up with the other.

I put my jacket over my head and tried to take our bearings. The surf was to our left, the knocking palms to our right. The wind was blowing in the direction of the village.

We ran for the village.

If the jungle had unnerved us by day, it horrified us in the pitch-black tempest. Wet fronds slapped our faces. We stumbled into knee-deep potholes filled with grasping mud. I tore my ankles on firethorns, my soles on limestone rock pinnacles.

At one point, I simply knelt down in the muck and begged Philip to give up, too, and die with me here, now.

That's when a blue sphere of lightning, no bigger than a basketball, shot out of the clouds and landed in the jungle about a hundred yards away. Every palm trunk, every individual hair on every palm trunk, the pores in Philip's blanched face, the stilt huts on the far side of the X-rayed trees, were all scored on my retinas. I shut my eyes in fear of going blind. The rumble of thunder that followed fractured over my cranium, as rushing water does over a rock.

We hurried toward the closest hut. Aside from the faint beacon of its cooking fire, we couldn't see anything, not even the tree-trunk ladder. I stumbled into it as one does an outstretched leg in a dark theater aisle.

The trunk was wet, the rungs slippery.

"I don't think I can climb it," I said.

"For God's sake, Sara, just go. I'll be right behind you."

He gave me a boost, and I clung and scraped my way up. I had no prior experience: East Side children never learn to climb trees. When I reached what I prayed was the top rung, Philip gave me a final heave, and I was at their front door.

All eyes were fixed on me as I crawled through the low archway into the smoky straw parlor. The occupants—a teenage boy with a harelip, a toddler, a mother and infant, and two young girls—sat huddled around a large stone bowl of flaring embers. The fire illuminated their faces from below, jack-o'-lantern–fashion.

"We lost our tent: it just blew away," I explained. "We're

very cold." I hugged myself to illustrate just how cold we were. "And we were almost struck by lightning. *Please,* may we stay?"

Philip crawled in after me. Even on his hands and knees, he crowded the already packed space with his sheer size—the whole house wasn't much bigger than a tenement parlor.

"We're friends of Ishmael's," Philip said. "Do you know him?"

Nobody appeared to recognize his Christian name, or if they did, no one said.

Another ball of lightning started its descent. Its trajectory was so brilliant and intense, it flashed through the bamboo walls and reversed the firelight. The red coals became dull gray, while the black shadows under our hostess's eyes turned incandescent.

Judging by the abrupt thunder, the fireball must have landed nearby.

The toddler put his hands over his ears and began whimpering. Over the diminishing booms, I thought I heard shouting outside. The young mother must have heard it, too. She handed her infant to one of the young girls, then stepped over Philip's outstretched leg and stuck her head out the door. When she drew it back inside, her hair was dripping and her face looked shocked.

Everyone heard the next scream. Thunder couldn't muffle it. Philip stood up. He almost punctured the low roof with his head. "Stay put. I'll be right back," he told me.

"I'm coming, too. Don't leave me here alone," I said.

The rain had turned to drizzle. The wind had died down to sporadic gusts. A branch of lightning struck the top of the mountains, but the thunder sounded faint. In the direction where the shouting had been, huts stood peacefully in shrouds of mist, save one: its roof was sparking, the fireball having been blown through its thatch.

Philip slid down the ladder, while I lowered my foot into the wet night, groping for a rung. I could smell fumes: a blend of metallic electricity, rank sulfur, and scorched straw. I could hear the sharp clang of metal striking metal. An iron church bell rung to summon help?

When I finally reached Philip's side, he was standing in front of the smoking hut along with a half-dozen other men. I recognized Ishmael. He kept his hand mashed over his mouth as he tried to fathom what had happened. When he noticed our runaway tent wrapped around the hut's roof, he turned his eyes on Philip and me. During the storm, our tent had evidently flown over the treetops, parachuted into the village, then jackknifed around the hut, catching on the eaves. It now hung in tatters, its cables clanging, a tent pole impaled in the scorched roof beside the smoking hole.

Philip and I were transfixed at the steel pole.

Ishmael hurried up the ladder, waving his arms to bat away the smoke. Three other men followed. When they entered the hut, we heard them choking. When they exited it, they couldn't stop choking.

The first body they lowered onto the ground looked as if it had been fabricated out of chalk. It even came apart like chalk. It left marks on the ladder.

The next body was smaller and obviously a woman's. I recognized the young breasts. From the throat up, the skin was covered in white ash. The tattooed bottom lip looked dusted with flour.

Ishmael sank onto his knees and pressed his brow against his granddaughter's, rolling his head from side to side. When he finally sat up, his face was covered in ash, too.

"I'm scared, Philip," I whispered. "I think we should leave."

"And go where?"

Two more bodies were pulled out of the smoke—a small boy's and a large dog's.

Philip took off his shirt to cover the boy's body, but Ishmael snapped the shirt out of Philip's hands and hurled it into the night. Ishmael then sank onto his haunches and locked his hands between his thin thighs.

"Ishmael," Philip said, "I'm so sorry for your loss."

Ishmael slowly turned around and stared at Philip. "Why did you come to my island?"

"We only came because we so admired your carvings."

Ishmael jerked his head sharply, as if to clear his ears of rainwater. "Because of my carvings?"

He opened his mouth again, then abruptly shut it and let his head fall forward until his chin scraped his chest. The rain varnished his back and shoulders until each tattoo shone with nuance and clarity.

What did grief look like under the splendor of these designs?

It looked exactly like grief.

The villagers came out of their huts and stood over the bodies. One tiny boy kept rubbing his eyes with his fists as if to screw them back into focus.

The Ta'un'uuans don't believe in acts of God. The idea that their deities would randomly and senselessly annihilate the innocent is inconceivable to them. Death is never random to the islander because it's never natural—lightning, fire, tidal waves, undertows, fevers, dysentery, even death by old age—none of it is natural. Death is always caused by your enemy, and if your enemy can't be seen or felt, then by a more insidious agent: your enemy's sorcery.

I looked around for Philip. Surrounded by a knot of angry young men, he was calmly and rationally trying to explain to them how the tent pole wound up on the burning roof. He used words like "velocity" and "chance."

I was more heedful of sorcery than he was. I was reared on the evil eye. A steel shaft in a flaming hut was proof enough for me of malignant forces.

I signaled Philip to slip away with me into the jungle, but he was too intent on convincing these men that there was a plausible explanation for the tragedy. He made an abrupt gesture with his hand to indicate our airborne tent.

One of the men took out a wooden knife and brandished it at Philip, then began muscling him toward what looked like a livestock pen. Philip cast his terrified eyes around for me. I ran over to the young mother who'd given us shelter during the storm.

"Tell them my husband was with you when it happened: tell them he isn't to blame. Tell them we were *both* with you when the fireball hit."

She acted as if she'd never seen me before.

I turned to Ishmael. He was still on his haunches, staring intently as a large fly feasted on his granddaughter's lip. "Ishmael," I said, "Philip sang for you and your granddaughter. We danced for you. You know we meant her no harm."

The old woman who had confronted Philip and me when we'd first come ashore was standing over Ishmael. I recognized her regal air. She silenced me with a vehement shake of her finger, then took me tightly by the wrist, as she might a child, and led me toward the livestock pens, too. I didn't resist. When she opened the stake gate for me, I actually said, "Thank you."

Philip was in the adjacent enclosure. Our stalls were made of bamboo staves. Six piglets shared mine. Philip's contained a huge hog with tusks. The hog was rooting through the folds of Philip's sarong to see if Philip had brought anything good to eat.

The guard watching over us almost laughed, then remembered the heinousness of our crime. He picked up a stick and prodded the hog into a thrashing fury. It kicked Philip on the thigh, then tried to bite his calf, but its tusks got in the way.

Finally, our guard threw down the stick and the hog calmed down. The man, however, didn't. He leaned over the gate and raged at Philip and me in one inexhaustible exhalation. Spoken anger in Ta'un'uuan sounds like a man blowing out a trick candle that won't die.

Philip sidled past the pig's tusks over to the far corner, then hunkered down into a protective ball. The hog was panting. I reached through the bars and touched his cheek. "You all right?" I whispered.

"I think so."

"Are they going to kill us?"

"I don't know."

"Should we try and run?"

"Where would you have us go?"

"The interior. We can hide in the mountains until the ship returns for us," I said.

"The mountains? We couldn't even assemble our tent properly. I'm going to try and reason with them, Sara. It wasn't our fault. They're human like us. They have to see that."

When the first pencil lights of dawn outlined the village, Philip arose to watch a group of men coming toward us. I stayed on my knees, peering through the bars. Ishmael was flanked by six ornamented, taut, eager young men, and trailed by a throng of villagers.

He opened the hog pen and addressed Philip in Ta'un'uuan. His wrath might as well have been the babble one hears before fainting.

Philip put up his hands as if he was silencing not a bereft grandfather but a vast noisy courtroom of jurors. With great passion, he started arguing our defense in the name of humanity. He continued arguing it as Ishmael ordered the warriors to lead Philip into the forest.

Dawn came and went. The sun flashed away all the puddles. The pigs were let out of the pens to sleep in the shade. Noon burned overhead. I was made delirious from the heat, frantic from thirst. Finally, the women came for me, the old woman accompanied by six female guards. Again, I followed her with something like gratitude.

She and the others led me into the forest in the opposite direction from where the men had taken Philip. The canopy's dampness felt sublime. I was allowed to rest now and again under a dripping tree, but when I opened my mouth to catch the leftover rainwater, she forbade me to drink.

We walked up and down footpaths, around bogs of black stumps, through partitions of ferns, until we came to a tall wooden structure in an overgrown clearing. It seemed to have been assembled entirely out of old European ship parts. The roof was an upside-down schooner hull, the rafters planks of bleached ribbing. Eight six-foot-high columns of mast held the hull aloft. There were no walls. The floor was decking.

The old woman led me under the boat and told me to lie down, faceup. I saw portholes brimming with daylight. Finally, she gave me something to drink, a bowl of what tasted like dishwater. I downed it greedily. When she offered me a second helping, I swallowed that, too. If it was poison, I wanted the quickest dose.

A physical inertia as close to divine serenity as I've ever known amassed in my limbs, pooled in my hands and feet. My head felt as hollow as a gourd. One would have had to have drunk a whole ocean of absinthe for this effect.

She poked my cheek with her fingernail: I couldn't flinch. She lifted my wrist, then let it drop: I couldn't jerk it away. She fed me another bowl, then got up and left, followed by the others.

I stared up at the ship. I didn't dare close my lids (the only muscles that still obeyed me). Whenever I did, I lost my footing on the deck, and was plunged into the open sea and left to sink in that cold vastness.

A minute or an hour later, Ishmael appeared under the ship's rail.

He was carrying pots of ink, and fish-bone pens, and I thought he was going to beseech me, as Philip had once beseeched me, to draw what I saw in my fever dreams. Instead, he knelt down behind me and unhurriedly examined his canvas. With both hands, he palpated my lips and chin. He said, or I hallucinated that he said, "You were so curious to own my art."

CHAPTER ELEVEN

Until I examined my face up close some thirty years later in the *Life* reporter's compact mirror, I could only imagine what Ishmael had inscribed on me.

Of course, I'd seen my visage over the years in rain puddles, in tidal pools, once in a mirror shard from a soldier's shaving kit that had washed ashore during the war, but for the full effect, both profile and dead-on, I had to wait for the reporter's pretty pink makeup mirror with its clever side panels.

When she offered me my first good look at myself in three decades, I asked to be alone. I sat down on the sand. Staring at the white-haired creature in the glass, I had so many other physical changes to contend with that the faded designs on my face seemed less than urgent.

The tattoos Ishmael engraved on my chin, on my lips, on the flesh around my lips are archetypical templates of the human mouth displaying fright, joy, shame, rage, rapture—the five quintessential expressions the Ta'un'uuans believe a face assumes over a lifetime, laid one atop the other. The result is the bottom half of a countenance so abstract it might as well be tree bark. The punishment is that the bearer of such a tattoo can no longer convey any sentiments of her own.

The procedure took days. The true genius of Ta'un'uuan tattooing begins with the dyes. Each color must be mixed anew every session from ingredients as scarce as insect wing dust, as rare as blue coral. For black, the islanders' most esteemed color—the "prince of color," as Manet called it—charcoal is fed to a dog. Its excrement is then mixed with candlenut oil and boiled down to a black as pure and permanent as engraver's ink.

The needles are fashioned out of human bone or tortoise-shell, then affixed to tiny bamboo rakes. The points are then dipped in ink and positioned against the skin. With a stone mallet, the artist strikes the rake, piercing the skin and inject-ing the ink deep into the dermis. By adjusting the needles incrementally after each tap, hundreds of dots are engraved every minute. Sometimes, for a thicker, truer line, the equiva-lent of an embossed etching, the skin itself is cut and the dye rubbed into the wound with a pepper leaf to promote scar-ring. When the pain becomes insufferable, the artist sings to his subject.

Ishmael never sang for me.

Each dawn, he arrived with his pots of freshly mixed ink, accompanied by the old woman. Sometimes another old woman appeared, too, but she sat at the far end of the hull, weeping.

Holding my head between his knees, Ishmael would work on a patch of my chin, or a turn of my lip, for the better part of the morning, while the old woman dabbed up my blood with bark cloths, then cleaned the incisions with poultices of leaves. When Ishmael finally set down his tools, she fed me my only nourishment, bowls of their dishwater elixir, through a hollow reed. My lips were so swollen that I couldn't open my mouth.

I presumed I was being readied for my execution, that the preparations entailed being mummified first in Ishmael's art, or perhaps he was merely inscribing my crime on my lips for all eternity.

When he and the old woman failed to come one morning, my gratitude at being spared the pain was qualified by my fear that only while my pain had lasted was I allowed to live.

I managed to stand up and walk to where the shade of the boat ended and the gas-flame-blue sky began. My jaw felt as heavy as an anvil, my cranium as light as helium.

Whenever I explored the area around my mouth (I couldn't help but touch it. Wouldn't you have been curious?), the skin felt as if it were smoldering. I knew I should run for my life—at the very least, crawl into the jungle and hide. I accepted that the next soul I saw would be my executioner.

Instead, I sat down and did nothing. I told myself I was too drugged and weak to flee, in too much pain to cope with the arduous demands of staying alive in the jungle. In truth, I think I preferred death to disfigurement.

Before the day was out, the old woman brought Philip to me. She led him by his wrist while he walked behind her. He could walk, though just barely.

The sun was setting at their backs. Philip was only silhouette and fiery outline. Even so, I could see they'd done something to his face, too. The old woman marched him closer. For a moment, he looked like my old Philip walking toward me under the striped shadows of the el train. She stood him directly before me.

Six bars—lampblack, ruler-straight—ran the length of his face.

"Sara, is that you?" he asked.

I couldn't make myself speak.

"I can't see." His eyes were swollen shut. (Even his eyelids had been tattooed.) He pawed the air, then turned his head from side to side. "They promised me you'd be here."

I stood and encircled his gaunt waist with my arms, pressed my brow—the only area of my face that didn't ache—against his chest and shoulder. I even kissed his throat with my swollen lips. "I didn't think I'd ever see you again," I said, though I couldn't make myself look at him as I said it. "I thought they'd killed you."

Then I stepped back to see exactly what they had done to him. The black lines started at his hairline (even his eyebrows were tattooed), ran over his features (even his nostrils were tattooed), and stopped at his jaw, eradicating everything that was Philip in between.

I was so muddled that I was sure the ink would rub off. I dragged my fingertip across his damp, striped forehead. When I lifted it off, I fully expected it to be smudged. It was clean.

"You're hurting me! Stop!" His voice emanated from the back of the cage. "Sara, I think Ishmael blinded me."

"You're not blind," I insisted; "your eyelids are swollen shut." I had no idea if it was true or not. I tried to muster a note of reassurance in my panicked, piping voice. "Try to open your eyes for me, darling."

He slowly cracked open his left lid; the right one was still too distended to lift.

"Do you see anything?"

"I think I see light." A sliver of his blue iris waffled back and forth, back and forth across the black stripe. "And outlines."

"Do you see me?"

The black lid fell shut. "It's too painful to keep open. Do you have any food, Sara?"

"Did you see me?" I asked again.

"I'm so hungry. They wouldn't give me anything to eat, just some kind of drug. Did they feed you? Are you all right?"

He reached out to touch my face as the blind do, but I dodged his probing fingers and held him by his wrists. I let him explore my eyes only. He palpated my closed lids, my brows, the tips of my lashes. "I couldn't bear it if they'd blinded you, Sara."

Something dropped on the floor behind us.

Philip jerked his head around. "Is she still here?"

The old woman was at the far end of the floor filling up a stone bowl with creek water. Two football-sized yams lay at her feet.

"Can she hear us?"

"I don't think so."

"Is she listening?"

"She can't hear us, Philip."

"I know what day it is." He lowered his voice to a conspiratorial whisper. "Sunday. At least, I think it's Sunday."

The old woman set down the bowl with a thud.

"Is she spying on us?"

"She's leaving us food and water."

"We have to get back to the camp, Sara. I kept track of the days. No matter what they did to me, I kept count."

The old woman padded past us down the stone steps and vanished into the jungle.

"Where's she going now?"

"I think she left."

"Tuesday. We are supposed to be picked up on Tuesday. Can you find the beach, Sara?"

I looked around me: jungle, jungle, and more jungle. I said I wasn't sure.

"You *have* to find that beach."

I said I didn't even know where we were.

"Follow the old woman."

"Now?"

"Yes, Sara, *now*. Her village is near our beach. At least I think it's near our beach."

I grabbed his hand to take him with me, but he wouldn't budge.

"I can't keep up."

"I'm not leaving you here."

"Sara, please, go before you lose her. Meet the ship. The captain will send men for me."

"I can't do that."

"For God's sake, don't you understand? They have a doctor on the ship. Maybe he can fix my eyes."

He then turned away from me and made the most familiar of gestures, an impassioned thrust of his head. It was the same gesture he employed at the crescendo of his old Alliance lectures to electrify us shopgirls into revolution. Now the gesture looked like something else entirely: now it looked like a man banging his head against the bars of his cell.

I crashed through shrubbery, stumbled over rocks and vines. I kept my hands in front of my tender face lest some branch thwack it.

The old woman had to have heard me. Wherever I stepped,

birds woke up and commenced shrieking. I left whole song lines in my wake. The sun was long gone, the ground slippery. She could have lost me if she wanted to. I could have lost myself.

Just as I spied the village's cooking fires, I recognized the path to our camp. At least I thought I recognized it. It was made of white coral, incandescent in the moonlight. A blind man could have found it. I walked until I felt sand underfoot. There was no wind. The ocean was flat. The storm had stripped all the fronds off the palms. The surf had reconfigured the beach into ramparts and dunes. Nothing looked familiar. I glanced around for remnants of our camp—the steamer trunks, the portable shower, our clothes, my paints. Gone.

For a minute or two, I thought I'd trekked to the wrong beach, that I was profoundly lost, that I'd die of thirst and starvation before anyone found me. Then a wand of moonlight glanced off a tin can rolling in the tide.

I ran to the water's edge and fished it out. The label was gone, but it had to be ours. Holding it to my ear, I gave a hard shake. Something edible sloshed within. I picked up a rock and started hammering. I was so hungry, I didn't care if I woke the whole village. I pummeled the can until the rock came apart in my fist. Then I picked up a bigger rock and whacked away. It fractured against the tin after two blows. Shaking the cylinder by my ear again, I became convinced I could actually hear which particular fruit was inside. Pineapple chunks! I kept shaking the can—frenetically, ravenously—in the hope that between my frustration and the internal pressure of the churning juice, the lid might blow. I found a jagged piece of coral and tried to saw through the hermetically sealed, unyielding seams.

At some point during the night, I must have given up and

lain down, because when I woke, it was already midmorning. The can was gone. A baked yam sat in its stead.

I didn't even bother to brush the sand off it. I ate it in fistfuls, as a toddler eats cake, then scanned the ocean for any sign of the *Pearl*. I walked the whole crescent of beach, squinting into the distance. I climbed onto the highest boulder and stood on tiptoe. A small white cloud shaped like a ship's smokestack drifted up out of the horizon and almost brought me to my knees.

When I looked again, the cloud was gone.

I sat down on the boulder, but every few minutes or so, I'd rise back up onto my tiptoes to peruse ship hulls that turned out to be glare, engine smoke that wafted away as haze. I kept telling myself the ship might appear any minute. It might already be Tuesday. Then again, it might be Wednesday or Thursday or Friday, and the ship long gone.

The sun reached its zenith. I drew the top of my blouse over the bottom half of my face to keep it from getting burned.

I would have wept, but I was too dehydrated.

When the smokestack cloud appeared once again, this time glimmering on the horizon to my east, I refused to put any stock in it.

For the next fifteen minutes or so, I watched as the tiny cloud changed from a smokestack into a waterspout, a rain curtain, an armada, a guano-stained rock islet, until the white shimmer finally stabilized as the prow of an ocean liner. Gulls were wheeling above it.

I got to my feet and started batting my arms above my head.

The ship was still miles away. No one on board, of course, could see me. At most, the beach was now only visible in the mate's binoculars.

I eased myself off the boulder, picked up the largest palm frond I could find, then hurried to the place on the beach where I figured I could best be spotted, on the highest, bone-white dune.

I didn't need to turn around. I knew the islanders were right behind me, watching my every move from within the forest. They'd probably spotted the ship long before I had.

I didn't make a sound or tense a muscle, lest I provoke them before someone on board had a chance to see me.

Only when the ship reached the outer reef, a mile at most offshore, only when the skiff was lowered into the water and the two sailors clambered aboard, only then did I wave my frond above my head like a football pennant and shriek.

The islanders didn't try to stop me. Quite the contrary. They ran onto the beach beside me, a hundred to my left, a hundred to my right. They were dressed in their full "welcome" regalia—foot-long penis gourds and straw skirts. A half dozen of the young men wore Philip's red-striped boxer shorts and my lace brassieres: they wore them as headdresses. Standing shoulder-to-shoulder on the dune's crest, they formed their great tapestry again, of which I was now evidently a panel. I was woven into the living cloth between the old woman and a warrior.

Everyone who could find a palm frond picked one up and shook it at the sailors in mimicry of me.

I threw down my frond and raised my arms to alert the sailors that I was the white woman for whom they were looking, and the islanders threw down their fronds and pointed to themselves. When I jumped up and down, shouting for the sailors to hurry up and rescue me, the islanders jumped up and down and shouted for the sailors to hurry up and rescue them.

When I finally broke ranks and plunged into the surf, screaming for the sailors to save me, the islanders ran into the waves, screaming for the sailors to save them.

From a hundred yards out, I doubt the sailors could distinguish one of us from another. My face, after all, was tattooed. I was practically naked. My hair, though red, was every bit as kinky as a Ta'un'uuan's.

All the sailors must have seen were screaming, gesticulating natives, of which I was merely the loudest and most hysterical.

They did not venture closer. They stopped and idled the skiff just outside the fringing reef. One scanned the shore with a pair of binoculars while the other wielded an oar, like a club, threatening the warriors not to swim toward them.

I was kneeling in the draining tide—sand-crusted, waterlogged, hoarse from shouting. I still thought I was distinguishable from the islanders, that all I needed to do to be rescued was to get the sailors to really look at me.

I rose up, streaming sea grass and salt water, and screamed till my throat went raw, and the Ta'un'uuans stood up and screamed, too.

The sailors shot off a flare. It corkscrewed across the low sky.

I suddenly remembered that Philip and I had been given a box of flares to signal back when the time came. I ran to the dune where I thought our camp had been and started clawing through the sand for flares. Without breaking ranks, the islanders ran with me, dropped to their knees, and searched, too.

To those on deck about to have their second afternoon cocktail, we probably looked like a flock of sandpipers hunting for crabs.

The sailors gunned the skiff, then slowly paralleled the shore, careful not to veer any closer. They both scoured the jungle with binoculars, stopping now and again to shoot off a flare.

The Ta'un'uuans and I watched as the flaming white tracers looped overhead.

When the sailors had practically circumnavigated the island, when they'd used up all their flares and still gotten no response, not even so much as a plume of signal smoke or a flash of mirror, they headed back to the ship and were hoisted aboard.

The ship blasted its horn and fired off a dozen more flares.

I stood atop my dune, waving my arms like a semaphore.

The islanders didn't try to mimic me any longer. They assembled on either side of me and watched intently as the ship let loose one last rocket before beginning its turn to the north. Only when it became clear to them that their audience was sailing away did they abandon their posts, and the great tapestry tore apart around me.

I sank down on the sand unable to take my eyes off the ship until it dissipated once again into vapor.

I found Philip just before dusk. It wasn't especially difficult. In my struggle to keep up with the old woman the night before, I had practically razed a one-lane highway across the island.

He was sitting where I'd left him under the vaulted hull. As soon as I stepped on the plank floor, he turned his head in my direction. I couldn't tell if he actually saw me or if he was merely following my footfalls.

I sat down across from him and placed my hand over his.

His thumb was torn and bleeding from picking at a splintery board while he'd waited. His left eye, the least swollen of the two, opened, just a notch.

"Where are the sailors?" he asked.

"You can see me, can't you?"

"Where are the ship and the sailors?"

"They wouldn't come ashore."

"What do you mean, they wouldn't come ashore?"

"When they didn't see us or our camp, they wouldn't come ashore."

"That makes no sense. How could they not see you, Sara?"

I tried to gauge, from the sliver of blue awareness behind the black bar, just how much he could see.

"Where are the sailors now?" he asked.

"They left."

"*They* left, or the *ship* left?"

"The ship."

"That's not possible. We're first-class passengers, for God's sake. Richter paid for our tickets. He's too important a man for them to just leave us here."

"They left us," I said.

"Of course they left us. They *left* to get help." He shook his head stiffly, but his voice reached a register he only hit when frightened. And, of course, I could no longer read his expression. It was like trying to decipher meaning in, say, a pattern of sunlight or the design on an insect wing.

"Someone has to come for us," he said.

He angled his head back the way a middle-aged man does when trying to focus on the fine print. His left eyelid drew almost completely open, then quickly shut.

"Did you see me?" I asked.

"I don't know."

"You don't know? Or you don't want to know?"

The lid slowly ascended. He looked straight at me.

"You see me, Philip. What do you think the sailors saw?"

CHAPTER TWELVE

Permanence is what gives the tattoo its power. A tattoo can't be torn up in a fit of artistic frustration, or undersold at auction, or tossed into a bonfire to make a point. It can't be dismissed by saying, "I'll do it better next time." Once written on the skin, a tattoo can never be undone, except, of course, by death.

Philip closed his one good eye and didn't open it again for the rest of the afternoon—whether to nurse it or to not look at me, I wasn't sure. He sat on the stone steps making frenzied, hopeless plans for our rescue, as if he could succeed where I had failed. First light, we'd walk back to the beach and *he'd* find the missing flares. Next, he'd build two tower-high signal fires on each end of the cove and one up on the cliff. After that, we'd circumnavigate the whole island and build a hundred more. "That's what you should have done, Sara, built a signal fire the second you reached the beach."

"With what?" I finally asked. "You have any matches? Because I sure as hell didn't."

He fell silent, then slowly turned around until he faced me. He opened his eye once again. "Do I look like a monster?" he asked.

I shook my head no, but so tentatively, it felt more like an admission than a denial.

"I need to know, Sara."

"There are just a few thin lines."

"Don't lie."

"Six. Stripes. Running down your face."

"Over my eyelids?"

"Yes."

"What color are they?"

"Black."

"Where do they begin?"

"At your hairline."

"End?"

"Your jaw."

"Are they thick?"

"Yes."

"You said *six*?"

"Six."

He gingerly touched his face as if he was trying to count them.

"What do I look like?" I finally asked.

He let his hands fall away. "They'll come off, Sara. Surely if they can build a skyscraper, they can remove our tattoos."

"What do I look like?" I asked again.

His good eye suddenly filled with tears. He tried to blink them back, but they spilled over onto his striped face. "Not so bad, really. You look like you're wearing a veil over your mouth."

"I didn't lie to you."

"Your lips are black. There are half circles on your chin and—"

"Stop looking at me!" I said.

I tried to cover my face, but he took hold of my wrists, then gently drew me against him until I stopped sobbing. By the time I quieted down, all that remained of the day were flashes of heat lightning in the twilight and a streak of molten sea where the sun had set.

We sat down side by side and waited for darkness to arrive as one would wait for a sedative to take effect.

Sometime during the night, I heard Philip stirring. I'd been too frightened to fall asleep myself. I groped for his hand, but I couldn't find it in the dark. There was no moon. The only hint of luminosity was the disks of stars visible through the hull's portholes.

"Sara, can you take me to the beach?"

"I can't even find your hand."

"We have to get back there as soon as we can and start a signal fire. We can use flint or bang together two sharp stones. A spark is all we need. If that doesn't work, we can always steal fire from the villagers. Captain Hirata wouldn't have just left us here. By now, he's radioed someone, somewhere, for help. We need to be on the beach first light so they can find us. Maybe he just moved the ship away from the reef for the night, anchored it up the coast, and you just didn't see him go there."

"I don't think he's anchored up the coast," I said.

"In any case, he'll never find us if we stay here." For a moment, his disembodied voice sounded so young and confident, so like my old Philip, that I almost gave in to it. Then I envisioned the black bars, and the bewildered wet blue eye looking out.

"I'm not sure I want to be found," I said.

"Don't say that."

"Are you so sure?"

He didn't answer me.

"How can we go home, Philip? Do you think we'll just resume our old life?"

"I don't know."

"Dinner with Richter at 21? Drinks in the Village afterward? How will we get there? Subway? Bus? Hail a cab?"

"I don't know."

"Who will stop for us?"

"I want to go home," he said.

First light, I guided Philip back to the beach. He still shuffled like a blind man, his good eye watering shut whenever the sun struck it. In the forest's shadows, however, I noticed that same eye managed surreptitiously to take in my profile.

I knew what he was looking for because whenever he rested his eye, I searched his face for it, too—the childhood scar, a flash of pink lip, anything familiar, anything to assure me that he was still inside.

About a hundred yards from where our camp had been, a fisherman stood knee-deep in the shallows, hauling in a net of undulating silver. He stopped to watch as Philip and I began dragging branches and logs out of the jungle and onto the dunes. He didn't seem at all alarmed that we were trying to build a signal fire. Matter of fact, when Philip and I couldn't incite so much as a hint of a spark by banging together two stones, he took pity on us, waded ashore and offered us a single match from a red and gold box he carried in his headband.

Staring down at the tiny matchbox stranded on his tattooed palm, I was so taken aback by the lettering—WASHINGTON

SQUARE HOTEL: *CONVENIENT TO EVERYTHING!*—that I almost forgot how it got there.

I would have given years to have kept that box.

Philip and I squandered the match in a draft of wind. The fisherman had to light our signal fire for us. As soon as he left, we stoked it until a thick plume of black smoke rose. Then Philip sat down to nurse his eyes. Cupping his hands over them to shut out the sun and smoke, he asked me to try and find him the same type of leaves the old woman had used as bandages. I stepped back into the jungle. None of the leaves looked familiar. I brought back an armful and let him pick.

I stood on the dune beside him and kept watch.

The sun continued its arc across the cloudless sky, the sea turned as flat as an ironed sheet, the horizon was a leaden pencil line dividing emptiness from nothing.

Around noon, thirsty, dizzy, desperate to spot something, I swore I saw the sky tear open and discharge a flying speck. I shrieked, "A plane! A plane!" But it turned out to be an albatross.

Philip finally removed the leaf poultices and tried to help me with the search, but he still couldn't focus on anything farther away than his outstretched hand.

We spent the night on the sheltered end of the beach, in a shallow cave notched into the base of a limestone cliff, huddled together spoon-fashion despite our sand-crusted, sunburnt bodies. We didn't dare lie face-to-face.

Two baked yams awaited us in the embers of our signal fire the next morning. We ate them in hot, tasteless fistfuls. That afternoon brought only a flock of white terns and an enormous gray pelican. The pelican landed on our diminishing woodpile, fluffed up its oily feathers, and surveyed the horizon with us. I think it was looking for its own kind, too. It only flew away when I tried to catch it for dinner.

Early the next morning, Philip's other eye opened at last. With both eyes working, he could measure distance, distinguish tint from shadow. If he squinted, he said, he could even make out some of the leaves on the trees. He insisted on standing first watch.

I retreated to the cool, dark shadows of the cave while he mounted the dunes, clad only in his sarong. It hung from his hip bones in tatters. A blond shadow had begun to bloom on his chin and cheeks, like moss on a black rock. Watching him train his swollen eyes with anticipation on the vapory distance only brought me despair and the breathless panic that goes with it. Not only was he about to see what I'd known all along—that our smoke signaled only the birds—but he was also able to see me plainly now.

By late afternoon, he was standing outside the cave. "They aren't coming back," he said softly.

I was against the wall where the sun never reached, where the sand was almost chilly. "I already know."

"What do you want from me, Sara? I was wrong."

He beckoned me to step outside, and when I wouldn't, led me out by my hand into the merciless sunlight. Picking up a stick, he sliced an X in the sand and said, "We're here." He then drew an outline of what I assumed was our island and made a dozen little pokes above it. "There are islets to the north. Maybe they thought we went there?"

"Why would they think that?"

"We'll die if we stay here."

"That's not true. They leave us food every night. There's plenty of water."

"We can't live on yams and water. Even if the *Pearl* left us here, they've sent out word. Every ship in the area must be looking for us by now. We're not that far from the shipping lanes. If we could just get past the reef, someone might spot us." The blue ellipses shifted in the black bars, then fixed on one of the fisherman's canoes, a hollowed-out log left on the beach.

"You know I can't swim," I said.

"We have no choice."

"Why not wait a little longer?"

"How much longer? Until they stop looking for us altogether?"

Just before dawn, we dragged the canoe down to the shore and pushed off at first light, paddling toward the milky blue channel in the reef. I must have back-paddled when he shouted "Fore," or stopped when he shouted "Go," because my half of the canoe entered the passageway sideways. When the first set of rollers broke over us, we tipped over. When the second set struck, I was shot down to the sandy bottom and sent tumbling into the reef. I opened my eyes to a blizzard of effervescence. I inhaled a lungful of water and tore my legs on the fiery coral. I lost all sense of up and down, solid or liquid, struggle or surrender. And just when numb serenity began to take hold, and I was certain I was home, the towering reef Manhattan's skyline, Philip grabbed hold of my hair and yanked me up into the shocking air. He half-dragged, half-carried me to the shore and laid me down on the wet sand, pummeling my back until I retched up seawater. He was shaking more than I was. He then lay down by my side in the draining tide and held me.

The sun had just cleared the mountaintops, and the water around us turned from red to tin to turquoise. Three fisherboys came out of the jungle and retrieved the canoe. It had washed up near the mangroves. They ferried it back to the shallows, then hauled it onto the beach.

My shins were gouged, my blouse was gone, my ankles scraped raw.

"Forgive me," he said.

"I got into the canoe as willingly as you did."

"For bringing you here."

After that, the only thing we cast into the waves was a daily missive, a coconut on which we'd carved our names and whereabouts, the date, September 1939, and the fact we were Americans and stranded. We were only five hundred miles east of British New Guinea, eight hundred northeast of Australia. The coconuts had to wash up somewhere, eventually.

Bare-breasted now, in my shredded linen pants, I worked on the lettering with a shell blade, while Philip, in the kerchief-sized remnant of his sarong, crushed a mix of berry juice and tree gum to dye the missives red so that they might catch the eye of the mate with the binoculars on the watch of a passing ship.

We were so depleted and dazed that we actually put stock in this plan.

Soon as a coconut was finished, Philip carried it along the

slippery base of the cliff and hurled it over the reef into the racing current. If he missed, though, the coconut got trapped in the surge for days, tossed up by the waves, slammed against the rocks. From my vantage point on the beach, it looked like a tiny red ball of hope being batted against a wall by a bored giant.

Nights, of course, I'd set sail in my dreams. Sometimes Philip was with me, sometimes he wasn't. The island would suddenly break free of its mooring on the ocean floor and drift east, float home. By next morning, it pulled right up to the Hudson piers, where a taxi awaited me. If Philip was along, we'd saunter down the bamboo gangplank arm in arm, miraculously dressed to the nines. Either our tattoos would have washed away in the salt air, or we could peel them off, like dead skin after a sunburn.

By Day Twenty-nine, awakening to find myself in the same dank cave, beside the same face that never failed momentarily to paralyze me, my only hope of rescue to carve my whereabouts on another coconut, I went berserk and bolted into the ocean, shouting for this to end, wanting to drown.

The tide was low. I ran for the exposed skyline of the reef. But when the first surge knocked me down and rolled over my head, I panicked and begged to live. The old woman appeared out of nowhere, grasped my flailing arms, and led me back to the beach.

I didn't even thank her, merely sank down on the wet sand. By the time Philip reached me, I was looking through him, as a catatonic looks through a wall. When he urged me to come back to the cave, to rest, at least to get out of the sun, his beseeching logic sounded, to my ringing ears, like Surrealist poetry. Finally, he left a bowl of water by my side and set off to collect wood for the insatiable appetite of our signal fire.

The sand turned from damp to warm to scalding. By midmorning, I was burned back to my senses. I rose up on bandy legs and turned around. My savior had multiplied into a half-dozen old ladies watching me from behind a fence of jungle. I could just make out their tattooed faces amid the veiny leaves.

When Philip trudged back under a stack of wood, I jerked my chin in their direction. He squinted at the exact spot where I'd pointed. "I don't see anyone," he said.

I regained the power of speech. "Are you blind?"

A frond shimmered and a cone of hair stuck out. A dozen more villagers materialized in between the palms to our left. Even Philip saw them.

"What do they want from us now?" I whispered. "Haven't they done enough to us already?"

"Maybe they're just curious? Maybe they've been watching us all along."

"Are we going to die here?"

"If they wanted us dead, Sara, they wouldn't have saved you."

"Maybe we are dead. Maybe this is hell."

For the next hour or so, we ignored them, hoping against hope that by pretending not to see them they might grow bored with us and go away, keep their distance as before without forgoing our daily ration of food—yams mostly, but now and then a breadfruit, or a bunch of sweet bananas, or a smoked silverfish that tasted, to me at least, like sablefish.

Philip fed the fire while I scratched away at another missive. But I couldn't concentrate. Now and again, a tattooed face peered at me from behind a fern and caught me unaware. It was as if I'd just glimpsed my own tattooed reflection in a flash of window glass.

By high noon, I couldn't stand it another second. I strode into the jungle and approached the old woman. She was standing in front of the others now, a general before her troops. I thrust my face in front of hers and stared back.

But you can't focus on a tattooed face for more than a second or two. The designs won't allow it. They swim apart, then bleed together. They ripple like wind on still water, then freeze like cracks of air through ice. Only when my vision blurred and I surrendered myself to the deep blue fissures under her flesh did I finally grasp that tattoos aren't written on the skin, they are written inside the skin. I wasn't looking at her tattoos, I was falling into them.

I finally had to shut my eyes.

When I opened them again, Philip was standing beside me. "She won't hurt you," he said. He was staring at her face, too. "I'm not sure if we're her prisoners or her pets, Sara, but I'm fairly certain she's the one who's been feeding us all along, the one who's been keeping us alive."

She motioned for Philip and me to follow her back to the village, but I couldn't move.

"Stay with me," I pleaded, but he had already started down the path behind her. I hurried after them.

The old woman had already climbed up onto the twelve-foot-high veranda of a stilted straw house by the time I reached the outskirts of the village. Philip was standing on the top notch of its trunk ladder. This house stood apart from the neat rows of other tree-high abodes, away from the pigs and the steaming earth mounds and the curious onlookers, at the base of a mountain. I hobbled over in my bare feet and Philip helped me up.

Through the low doorway, in the center of the smoky room, a man knelt over a woman, his back to us. He had been painted all over with white clay. Even the soles of his tattooed feet had been painted out with clay. The woman beneath him, a bag of bones, lay supine. Her head had been shaved.

The ladder creaked and the clay man spun around. Despite his white mask, I recognized Ishmael.

The woman on the floor also turned her head to stare, but I doubt she saw us. Her eyes looked as dead as marbles. I recognized her, too. She was the woman who had quietly wept in the corner while Ishmael and the old woman had worked on my face. She closed her eyes. Without the obscuring marbles, she looked just like her dead granddaughter.

Turning his attention back to his wife, Ishmael pressed his brow against hers and began singing, as if to woo her back to life with his voice. Bowls of ink surrounded them, a needle was in his hand. Exhaling one long note, he dipped the needle into the pot of indigo and brought it dripping to her throat, but he didn't incise her. He simply painted in the gouges she'd already made with her own fingernails. You could see she'd been tearing at her skin for weeks. Raw lines ran down her neck. Under the barely healed scars, strings of indigo and turquoise, yellow and viridian were visible. In places, her scarred neck was so covered in bright, festive threads that it looked as if Ishmael had been trying to stitch her grief closed with pure color.

"We should leave," I whispered. "Leave them alone."

I tried to take Philip's hand, but he wouldn't come with me.

When I stumbled down the ladder, he didn't even turn around. I left him transfixed on the top rung and made my way back to the cave alone.

Philip returned just as dusk fell and lay down beside me, he and I face-to-face for the first time since we'd been given our new countenances. We hadn't so much as kissed once in all those weeks. The sun was gone, but there was still more than enough light to see by.

He took my hand and pressed it against his face. "Touch me, Sara. I won't survive if you don't touch me," he said.

I ran my hand lightly over the black bars.

I could feel him tremble.

I caressed his throat and chest, but he took hold of my wrist and stopped me. "I need you to mark me."

"Don't say that, Philip. *That* scares me."

He guided my hand over to the cold ashes left by our cooking fire and dipped my fingers into the soot. "Do this for me," he said.

I made a few timid smudges on his shoulders to appease him, then tried to get him to make love to me, but he wouldn't let go of my wrist.

With his hand guiding mine, I ran my blackened nails lightly down his front, over his stomach and groin. When his grip finally slackened in surrender, I tugged myself free and covered his entire lower abdomen with ash, gray wavelets of empty ocean. Next, I ran my finger around his thin waist and drew a horizon, thick as a belt, to cinch my ash sea to the sky and keep the waters from falling away. Beneath the horizon, I drew the skyline of Manhattan. I then dusted my own face with soot and pressed my cheek and chin and lips against his, imprinting my profile on his face. I poured a fistful of ash into the coconut shell we used as a drinking cup and stirred it around until my fingers were black. I then began brushing it across his chest in the tiny silhouette of a ship. Nothing elegant, nothing at all like the *Pearl*. Just the hull of the proverbial ship on the horizon, the one every castaway waits for, the one we're all waiting for.

CHAPTER THIRTEEN

All that remained of my drawings the next morning was a dusting of ash on Philip's skin, except for two remarkably intact images—the black ship on his chest and the pale stigmata of Manhattan's skyline rising out of his lower abdomen. On my own flesh, there were faint traces of those images in reverse from when he had finally held me against him during the night, made love to me, then wouldn't let go.

We dressed, he in his tatter of sarong, me in my shredded boy's pants, and stepped out of the cave just as dawn broke. The old woman and her cronies were already waiting for us by the trees, though they no longer bothered to conceal themselves. They walked up to Philip and surrounded him. I could see how intrigued they were by my drawings. Their general, our keeper, stepped front and center to examine my work in close-up. She scrutinized the ship and the skyline. Then, stepping back, she turned around and faced me, glancing down at the smudge of ship between my breasts, then at my blackened hands. Her tattooed brows rose up. She turned back to Philip and rubbed her fingertip lightly across my ship; the hull smeared in two. She ran it over the skyline: the tops of the buildings were wiped away. She examined her blackened fingertip, then held it up for the other ladies to inspect. They gaped at it as if it had been dipped in blood.

I couldn't tell how much of her act was theatrics and how much was genuine shock at the primitiveness of our methods, but when she finally looked back at Philip and me, I swear I saw something that resembled pity for us beneath the maze on her tattooed face, inside her skin.

She walked back to the village, trailed by the others.

That afternoon, our daily allotment of food was left on a flat rock by the cave's mouth. She must have put it there while we were napping. In addition to our regulation yams, she'd included a red hairy fruit that tasted like perfumed apples, two green bananas, one fish, a dollop of ambrosial honey wrapped in a banana leaf, and a set of tattoo needles—turtle shell, shark tooth, and bone.

I couldn't make myself touch the needles.

On the next rock over, four stone pots of ink had been set in a circle. One contained the exact metallic blue-green shade an ancient copper dome turns when the sun strikes it. Another held what looked like purple squid ink. A third seemed to be filled with pulverized red orchids. And the fourth, black: it wasn't mixed from an absence of color, it was mixed from the bounty of colors.

Kneeling, his long uncombed hair looking like the blond batting used to stuff sofas, his thin torso adorned with nothing more than smudges now, Philip gaped at the pots of liquid radiance. The inks were *that* beautiful.

He picked up the needle made of bone. It was a little longer than his finger.

"Put it back," I said.

He ignored me.

"I don't want it in my house," I said.

He turned it over in his hand. All up and down the narrow shaft were minute carvings of copulating figures.

"What house, Sara? We have no house. No clothes. No shoes. No matches. No faces. No one is coming for us." He shook his head from side to side: the moving bars gave me vertigo. "We'll lose our minds if we keep staring at the horizon."

"It hasn't even been two months. You have to give the coconuts a chance."

He spun me around until I faced the ocean—emptiness to the north, emptiness to the south, water to the left, water to the right. A red coconut was being pummeled against the reef.

He turned me back again, then drew me against him. "We were happy last night." He pressed my hand against his chest.

My fingers were still sooty enough to leave a faint mark. I drew a lightbulb on his shoulder, a beacon for the ship to steer toward. When I finished, though, the lines were so light that even I could hardly see them.

He took hold of my hand again and guided it over to the closest pot, dipping my fingertips into the ink. They came out copper-blue. I started painting over the breaches the old woman had rent in my ship's hull: the blue ink only made it look as if the hull was taking on water.

Philip lightly supported my drawing wrist in one hand, while his other dipped the bone needle into the blue pot and carried it dripping back to me.

But I wouldn't take it. "Please don't go mad on me, Philip. Don't leave me here alone."

He wouldn't release my wrist.

"I could hurt you. I could disfigure you," I said.

"You can't disfigure me any more than I already am."

He sat back on his heels and pulled me down, too. It was just before sunset. The sun's rays were horizontal. They pierced the cave's wide mouth and irradiated the limestone walls. The cave was as bright as an operating theater.

"It'll never come off," I said. "You may come to hate it. You may come to hate me for it."

"I could never hate anything you drew."

He offered me the needle again and I took it this time. After all, I was just as curious as he was. He stretched out on the rock floor and shut his eyes: without his blue eyes, I had nothing with which to orient myself that this was Philip. The black bars gave way to the blond beard, which in turn gave way to the long thin sunburnt canvas below me. "Tell me what to draw," I said.

"It doesn't matter. Anything you put on me is already inside me. Draw what you see."

I shut my eyes, but there was no Surrealist theater on the back side of my lids. There was nothing but emptiness. When I opened them again, all I saw was my sinking ship. I put the needle to his chest at the hull's prow and pushed the ink inside. I felt him wince and stiffen.

"It doesn't hurt me," he said.

I moved the needle a millimeter down the keel and pushed again. A minuscule ruby of blood came out. I made the next pinprick with my eyes averted, and kept them averted each time I jabbed. Only when my fear subsided and I was able to look at the blood as I was drawing it was I able to glean what we were doing.

The Ta'un'uuans believe that to tattoo and to be tattooed is the deepest form of intimacy—the puncturing of the skin, the entry into another's body, the flow of blood, the infliction of pleasure and pain, the closure and healing of the wound, and most of all, lest anyone forget, the indelible trace of the process.

Where we in the West believe that our true selves, our unsullied psyches, the secret cores of our being, are buried deep beneath our façades, hidden from others, hidden sometimes even from ourselves, the islanders believe that their true selves are written on their skin, on every point and place where one human being connects to another.

By the time the sun had set, all Philip and I had managed to accomplish was the barest outline of the hull. It wasn't even watertight. He wanted me to continue by firelight, but I couldn't see anything.

Next morning, his tattoo had hardened into a translucent scab, my blue engraving just visible under the crusted skin. Philip sat up. Head bowed, neck twisted, his blond beard scraping against his breastbone, he shut one eye to better focus on the tiny tattoo below. I wasn't sure just how much of it he could see from that angle, but from where I lay, on the hard sand by his knees, I saw a rapt blue eye looking out of a birdcage at a toy ship.

When we finally stepped out of the cave, the old woman and her coterie sat waiting for us. Within seconds, they spotted the raw tattoo on Philip's chest, noticed that my fingers were stained not just with ink, but with dried blood. We walked past them to squat in the high grass. They discreetly turned away and lowered their eyes. I think they finally grasped that the beleaguered, half-mad, helpless creatures living in a cave on their beach were human like them.

That afternoon, a couple of dozen men appeared in the tall grass on the sheltered end of our beach. They bore five full-length palm trunks on their shoulders and carried long, thick bamboo stalks in their hands. Here and there, a flash of sun would glance off an ax blade slung from the same string belt that held erect a penis gourd. They set the trunks down in the shape of a star, then unslung their axes and hacked away at the stubborn grass until they'd cleared a perfect circle. They made a human scaffold, three men tall, to stand the trunks up, while the skinniest boys clambered up the sweating bodies to pound on the top of the posts with skillet-sized flat rocks. As soon as four of the trunks were firmly planted in the ground, and a rudimentary platform erected, the men reconfigured them-selves into a hive and began assembling the bamboo stalks into a bowed armature that looked, to me, like a giant's rib cage. It was tall enough for me to stand up in. They then tied the curved trusses to the straight crossbeams with knots so complex they would have baffled sailors. Next, the strongest of the men hoisted the cage onto their shoulders while the skinny boys, biting the ends of long ropes, shimmied up the palm trunks. Hand over hand, they somehow managed to raise the rib cage atop the platform and anchor it to the wooden posts with iron nails. Finally, unstringing their axes once again, they chopped out footholds in the one remaining palm log and leaned it against the stilted structure, like a staircase. Only then did I realize that they were building Philip and me a house with the penny nails and steel axes we'd purchased only months before at a bargain outlet on the Lower East Side—*I remember!*—Goldberg & Sons Discount Hardware at the corner of Delancey and Essex. The next day, the women joined the work party, carrying bundled straw for the roof atop their heads, while the men, in slow relays, labored under a ten-foot-long sandalwood roof beam. Even Ishmael helped carry it.

Philip and I slept in our new house that night though it wasn't quite finished. It had no door and only half a roof. It smelled of sawdust and hay. A high-borne breeze wafted through the reed walls and kept the mosquitoes away. We hardly had anything to pack and move—a driftwood walking stick, a shell knife, three shell spoons, two coconut canteens, two coconut bowls, Philip's shred of sarong and my linen pants, the one sandal we still had between us, and the four stone pots trembling with liquid pigment and the tattoo needles.

CHAPTER FOURTEEN

In a typical day, the old woman would wake us at first light, shouting up from the beach below for me to follow her to the dripping tiered gardens, Philip to accompany the fishermen in their canoes. She had us call her "great-aunt," as all the villagers did, but when I made a mangle out of the Ta'un'uuan words, she let me call her by her Christian name, Laadah. Under her strict tutelage, I was taught the skill of planting taro shoots (the trick is to feed them bat guano), while Philip was instructed by the fishermen in the art of net throwing. He even learned how to hurl a three-pronged spear into a jackfish.

When the heat of the day spiked and the soil began steaming, Laadah would set down her hoe, and I'd follow her to a sunken limestone spring garlanded with hanging orchids. Usually, a dozen other ladies would already be soaking in the cool water, gossiping, the bawdier the incident the louder the laughter. I might not have spoken their language yet, but their lascivious pantomimes made their punch lines abundantly clear. When the water finally chilled us, we'd dry off in the sun, then perfume ourselves with orchid petals (the white ones smelled like vanilla) and rendezvous with the men back at the village to eat the midday meal in one noisy congregation.

Philip and I usually dined on the fringes of Laadah's extended family, a pandemonium of nieces and nephews and second cousins and poorer relations that seemed to include, at one time or another, practically everyone in the village.

For the most part, the Ta'un'uuans' culinary skills consist of dropping tubers into a fire, though once in a while Laadah and the women outdid themselves and prepared a collective feast of tapioca pudding and honeyed pork that rivaled any one-star restaurant. They had me work as a prep chef.

A half hour or so after we ate, a mass drowsiness overtook the village. Stupefied families hauled themselves up to their tree houses and sank into communal hammocks. Even the pigs fell to snoring.

A mile away, in the shade of our own straw roof, Philip would lie facedown or supine, depending upon which side of him I was tattooing, while I lined up my needles and inks, all the while appraising his abdomen or chest or buttocks anxiously.

I don't mean to suggest that I was tattooing Philip from head to toe. Quite the contrary. In those first few months, whole afternoons passed and we'd barely advance an inch.

It took me three full sessions just to master the insertion of the needle without spilling any color beforehand. It took me another six to learn the art of the comb and mallet: how to forcefully tap the comb's back so that all six needles entered the skin simultaneously. And it's taken me almost thirty years to finally grasp the true complexity of the Ta'un'uuan palette. Mixing color on a canvas is one thing, mixing color under the skin is quite another. I had to master both the chemistry of the body and the absorbency of the flesh.

I finished the ship first, made it as watertight as my fledgling skills allowed, then proceeded to engrave the erratic graph of Manhattan's skyline across his lower abdomen. I wasn't yet confident enough to try anything unplanned.

When the pain became too much for Philip, he'd grab hold of my drawing hand and not let go. Sometimes he'd kiss it afterward; sometimes we'd make love. In any case, sex or no sex, we'd both lie back, spent.

Invariably, the day's end would find us on the beach. Philip's beard had grown voluminous; his hair reached well below his shoulders. My tattoos now covered his right biceps, his right buttock, and a large patch of chest. He wore a penis gourd and a string belt the fisherman had given him. They even performed a little ceremony to show us how to tie the foot-long gourd in place: the testes are left to dangle. All that remained of my linen pants were three wooden buttons. I traded them for a grass skirt.

Sitting side by side on the warm sand, our shoulders brushing, we'd watch the sunset. Even the islanders quit whatever they were doing to show respect for the end of the day.

At the precise moment the sun goes down, color becomes its richest. For less than an eye blink, the white disk of the sun turns copper green and pulls all the light down with it. You could be sitting on an open beach or in your darkening living room: all edges disappear. The maroon sky and the maroon sea are one. And every object floating against that emptiness—the blue-violet clouds, the cinnabar lichen on the wet rocks, the blond canoe on the sand—becomes the brightest object on earth.

It's these final seconds of twilight that have inspired the Ta'un'uuan palette.

· · ·

The tattoo on the small of my back was etched during those afternoons. It's the only tattoo that Philip ever gave me, though I offered him my body countless times. He chose the one spot for it where he knew I wouldn't be able to see it, or judge it.

I saw it for the first time in a Saks Fifth Avenue changing room. *Life* had practically whisked me there straight off the airplane to photograph me in my first new dress in three decades.

Seeing myself in a three-way mirror, the full display on my back obscured only by the brassiere strap that a salesgirl had helped me fasten, left me speechless. When she and the *Life* reporter poked through the curtains to hand me an armful of dresses and suggest that the hyacinth-pink one might be the most flattering shade with my complexion, I merely nodded.

Several inches below the strap, encircled by my own later designs, Philip's tattoo seemed wholly artless in its intent. It's a simple self-portrait, without the bars.

Just when it seemed that there was no other reality but this one, no other world beyond the horizon—that Philip and I must have dreamed up New York, electric lights, the art world, ironed sheets, iced martinis—just when it occurred to me that we hadn't discussed plans for our rescue in weeks, months, and that we might actually be happy here, we awoke to find our beach from the mangroves to the cliffs awash with what looked like East River refuse: tin cans, glass bottles, twisted sheet metal, tangles of black wires, bloated wood chunks, a piece of rubber raft, a quarter moon of life preserver.

"Are we hallucinating?" I asked.

"Why would we hallucinate garbage?"

He slid down the ladder and sprinted over to the nearest pile. It was scattered along the high tide mark, fifty feet from our door. He picked up what looked like a canteen and turned it over in his hands. It was definitely aluminum. It blinded him momentarily with a flash of mirrored sunlight. Shielding his eyes, he stared out at the horizon, then up at the sky.

I automatically looked, too. There was nothing out there. I was still on our balcony, the windward side, trying to get an overview of the cove. Legions of gulls were wheeling above the refuse.

Behind me, from the forest, I could hear voices, branches snapping, the whoosh of grass skirts. The whole village was coming through the trees, the children first. A night fisherman must have alerted them about the refuse, or perhaps the Ta'un'uuans have a sixth sense and the cargo had washed up in their dreams.

Philip began picking his way along the water's edge—a dented can, an iron rod, a piece of rubber tarp. The children caught up to him, grabbing what they could, whipping each other with phone lines and laughing.

The adults were hurrying beneath me now, wide-eyed babies jiggling in their mother's arms. Laadah and the other old women were a few yards behind. Ishmael and a warrior stepped through the ferns choking the coral path. The man's arm was still bleeding where Ishmael had tattooed it.

Down the shore, a night fisherman beached his canoe and began wading into the mangroves.

I climbed down the ladder and joined a knot of women tightening around a gunnysack of rice. We knew it was rice because it bore a picture of rice. It also bore Japanese calligraphy and a red sun. A woman and I reached for the sack simultaneously. We actually got into a tug-of-war. A few feet to my left, three warriors almost came to blows over a khaki knapsack, and to my right, a pubescent girl coveted what looked like a lipstick tube in her tiny fist, while her two friends tried to pry open her clenched fingers. Beyond them, bounding across the sand, the village stragglers had just arrived. They pressed against us, staring at our treasures, their faces wet and shiny from running. Butterflies had followed them and now landed on their cheeks and brows, drinking their fill of human sweat.

I heard a woman shriek, or maybe it was a gull. They were dive-bombing around us, wings batting, picking up spilled rice. Pigs were rooting by our feet.

Philip, thronged by the laughing, dervish children, looked for the source of the scream.

Laadah and the old women were walking toward him, parting the melee of grabbing hands. Laadah let out an even more shrill shriek. Everyone fell still and set down what they were clutching. Having gotten the villagers' attention, she mounted a dune, threw back her head, opened her mouth, unfurled her blue-black tongue, and broke into song. She held her raspy notes as long as her lungs allowed.

Finally, one of the warriors picked up the knapsack and offered it to her. She held it up to her eyes, twisted it, pulled it, smelled it, then passed it to the other old women crowding around her. The girl brought her the lipstick tube. Weighing it in her ancient palm, she took counsel with the others: you had only to look at their faces to see the alarm.

I pressed my way toward Philip. He was now on his knees, examining a second lipstick tube. I grabbed it out of his hands. It was a bullet. Even I, who had never seen one up close before, knew what it was.

The boy beside me held up a handful of weightless pure white plastic foam, the innards of a life jacket. We all gaped at it as if it were snow. It looked so beautiful.

The children started shrieking again, even louder than the gulls. We all looked in their direction. A truck tire had just washed ashore. The man beside me went slack-jawed. It wasn't like seeing an inner tube float onto the beach with the beer bottles at Coney Island. This tire had come to a shore where the wheel had yet to be invented. The awe on my neighbors' faces wasn't goggle-eyed primitivism; it was reverence.

The islanders surrounded it. They had to touch it for themselves. When Philip and my turn came, we examined the raised lettering on the sidewall, the same Japanese calligraphy as on the gunnysack.

It took no time for the children to master the art of tire rolling. They pushed it back and forth, over the dunes, in between the adults, until the elders took it away and had two warriors roll it to the village. Everyone followed, picking up as much as they could carry—copper wires, fistfuls of rice, hunks of flapping sheet metal, a jackboot, a glass bottle, another bullet. What the first vanguard couldn't manage was picked over by their cousins. What their cousins couldn't haul was seized by the village stragglers. What they abandoned was rooted through by the pigs. What the pigs couldn't find was pecked over by the gulls. What the gulls didn't see was savored by the sandpipers.

To any ship that might be searching for the sailor who had worn the life jacket, our cove now looked as primeval as ever.

Philip and I had grabbed what we could, too—the now empty rice sack, the bullet, a piece of rubber raft, a knotted white bandanna, what looked like the broken-off end of a machete blade—and laid them out on our balcony.

"I don't think they've been in the water long," Philip said, examining the bullet. He used his thumbnail to scrape off any flecks of corrosion on the casing. "It's barely begun to rust."

"How long does it take something to rust?" I asked.

"In salt water? Not very long."

"A day? A week? A month?"

"Not long enough that they would have called off a search for survivors."

I picked up the broken blade. It was longer than my forearm. "Survivors of what?"

"I think that's a bayonet," he said.

He untied the sopping bandanna. He had to use his teeth. It was double-knotted and looped to fit around a forehead. When he opened it at last, I saw a Rising Sun.

"A Japanese ship must have gone down near here," he said.

"Maybe the tire came from a plane?"

"It has to be a ship. We're hundreds of miles from any air route."

"What kind of ship? They didn't have bayonets on board the *Pearl*, Philip."

"Maybe it was a navy ship."

"Why would it come here?"

"Maneuvers. Exploration. They have colonies in the Gilberts. Maybe it was a merchant ship and the bayonet was just cargo?"

"Who would they send bayonets to, in the middle of the ocean? They're fighting in China."

"Maybe the ship was lost, Sara. Does it matter? Ships travel in convoys. There might be others out there. We have to get the fires started again."

"We don't have to," I said.

"You can't be serious."

"Aren't you happy here?"

"We can't stay here."

"Why not?"

"Because it's not real."

That afternoon, he rebuilt the fires. He even climbed up to the crag on the cliff's face to relight the woodpile we'd once kept burning there.

I had no choice but to assist him. I trekked through the forest gathering wood. Each time I neared the village, I smelled roast pig, heard singing. Once I even heard flutes. Tens of them. I peeked through the trees. The men sat in a circle, chanting in their subterranean baritones. The women crouched in a separate circle, blowing on the rims of glass bottles, playing the strangest scales I'd ever heard. Some of the bottles had washed up this morning, but others looked very old: the glass had clouded. The children ran wild. Everyone had ornamented themselves with found objects—a bright metal pipe for a penis gourd, a bullet for a nosepiece. One young woman had wound a long piece of copper wire around her neck until it looked like the neck of a lightbulb. When she spotted me, she smiled and waved for me to come sit beside her.

Tempted as I was, I lugged the wood back to Philip and told him about the invitation, the musical bottles, the roast pig, that we'd been asked to join the celebration, that it would be rude not to.

"I want to go home, Sara."

He went off to start another fire, this one facing south. I couldn't very well abandon him. I made myself useful by keeping a lookout for ships, even though I wasn't sure I wanted to be rescued. Yet each time a cloud changed shape on the horizon, I became as spellbound as he.

We worked through the night, taking turns feeding the fires.

On my watch, a couple appeared on our beach for a moonlit tryst amid the dunes. They saw our fires raging on both ends of the cove, another up on the cliff. I heard them whispering. I think they assumed that the fires were our way of paying homage for the cargo.

The next morning, Laadah called us to work as usual. We feigned fevers, but she was hardly fooled. Half the village had played hooky to scour the shoreline for anything else that might have washed up during the night.

Philip and I spent our day hauling wood.

On the third morning, he wanted us to ferry burning torches across the murky mangrove swamp so that we might set a new ring of blazes on the windward shore.

"I won't do it," I said.

"Won't *what*? Cross the swamp? Carry a torch? Save yourself?"

"Hope."

For the next few days, I hauled my share of wood, stood my share of watch, but whenever I walked the shoreline alone, I kept my eyes fixed on the sand between my feet. I never wanted to see another chimerical cloud again.

That's when I found it, the soldier's shaving kit, half-buried in the wet sand. It must have just washed up, or someone would have snatched it by now. A crab scuttled out. Then another. The kit was filled with sand. I poured it out and began sifting through its contents, blindly, wildly. Something cut me, a shard of mirror no bigger than a thumbnail. I set it on my palm, blew off the film of sand, then lifted it up to my face and looked just long enough to see that I didn't want to look *that* closely, and flung it back into the sea.

CHAPTER FIFTEEN

The whale appeared a week later, on the far side of the barrier reef, erupting out of the swells.

I was on the dunes, collecting turtle eggs for breakfast. The night fishermen had just paddled ashore. They spotted the colossal gray shape before I did, dispatched a fisherboy to alert the village, and then pushed off in their canoes again. The whale must have been sixty feet long.

The blowhole opened and a man climbed out. I started shouting for Philip. The boy stopped in his tracks. Five more men climbed out of the hatch.

Philip must have heard me because he was halfway down the ladder, staring at the submarine. He dropped to the ground, grabbed an armful of dried-up fronds and coconut husks, and ran past me toward the closest fire. He threw the husks on top, then lit a frond and began waving the flaming fan above his head, trying to shout over the hammering surf.

The men on deck didn't respond. The ship was a half mile out. The sun had just cleared the treetops. The entire sky was crimson. Our fire must have looked like a candle flame flickering before a floodlight.

"They can't see us," Philip said. He threw down the frond. "We have to make them see us."

"Who are they?" I asked.

"They're from our world, Sara." He was looking up and down the beach for something else to use as a signal.

"Maybe we should wait for the others," I said.

"They'll leave if they don't see us."

He ran back to the house and brought out the bayonet. Standing on the edge of the balcony, he tried to angle it so that its steel blade caught the sun's rays and flashed an elementary SOS. But the sun was directly behind him now. Even I couldn't see the glints, and I was only a few yards away.

"Bring me a burning branch," Philip shouted.

I pulled a stick out of the fire, and brought the fledgling flame to Philip, carefully cupping it in my hands as I walked. It almost died out a half-dozen times. He grabbed it out of my fist, hurried up our ladder, then held it up to our straw roof.

"What are you doing?" I said. "It's our home, Philip."

Without lowering the flame, he moved methodically around the eaves, torching all four corners.

The fire began crawling skyward. He slid down the ladder and pulled me clear of the house. The eaves reddened, the bamboo rafters shook violently, then the entire roof exploded into flaming straws that rained down on us.

The men on board saw *that*. They waved and shouted to those below.

The swiftest of the villagers, young men mostly, were already coming through the trees, adorned for the whale hunt in their prize finds—bullet nosepieces, copper-wire armbands. They raced toward the sea only to stop short when they spotted the men on the spine of the steel whale, men who had the sorcery to master a monster.

Holding fast to their harpoons, they hooded their eyes and squinted at the hybrid of ship and fish. Philip joined them at the waterline, holding the bayonet over his head, flashing the blade again so that sailors would see that there *were* survivors present, if not from last week's shipwreck, then from another disaster.

The sailors unlashed a rubber boat from the deck and heaved it into the sea. Ten more men climbed out of the hatch and everyone scrambled aboard, save for the man giving orders.

Philip reeled around, looking for me. I was standing by the ruins of our house. It now lay in a heap of smoking thatch.

"They're coming for us, Sara! We're saved!"

The next throng of villagers had just arrived, young women and children kicking up sand as they ran. They, too, had bedecked themselves for the hunt. One tall thing had powdered her hair with the life jacket's innards until it was as white as a barrister's wig. Another had knotted a Japanese bandanna around her waist. When the women and children spotted the sailors motoring shoreward, they began assembling themselves into their "welcome" tapestry. They left spaces for their elders.

The boat was now riding the breakers over the reef, but the waves kept crashing short. It almost capsized. It fishtailed sideways, then rocketed forward. I could now make out the wet, frightened faces of the sailors on board. They looked like the shy Japanese cabin boys who'd served us afternoon tea on the *Pearl.*

Philip shouted for the sailors to watch out for the sandbar. It was directly before them. He fervently pointed to the danger with the bayonet, and the young fishermen up to their thighs in sea water beside Philip brandished their harpoons as pointers, too.

The bottom of the boat hit the sandbar and the sailors were tossed about. When they regained their balance, the sailor steering the skiff stood up and pointed at Philip and the charging young men.

Philip was out front, shouting that we were Americans, steamship passengers from a Japanese vessel, that we'd been marooned here for almost a year. He cried out my name and his, and the young men cried out their names, too.

The sailors lifted their rifles and fired.

Most of the men were up to their armpits in water. They didn't fall backward. They simply sank beneath the surface. Those left standing blinked mechanically at the spot where their brothers had vanished. The only sounds were the surf and the whine of the boat's propeller. The birds had fallen mute.

All at once, the bodies floated up. Most bobbed facedown, but a few were thrashing.

I looked for Philip. He wasn't among the standing. I searched for his blond hair in the water. The sea was darkening with blood.

The gulls started shrieking again, and the cockatoos exploded out of the trees, and the women and girls wailed. Those with children swooped them up and ran for cover. I couldn't make myself move. Ishmael and the other old men had only now reached the beach. They, too, had ornamented themselves in bullets and talismans. When they saw their felled sons, one or two covered their mouths in anguish, while the rest hurried toward the sea.

I threw myself onto the sand.

The sailors took aim and fired again. The first line of old men fell on the beach near me, fifty feet short of their sons. Ishmael simply sat down, one foot folded under him, and stared curiously at the spot where the bullet had entered his stomach, rupturing his design. Each time he exhaled, a bubble of blood distended from his open lips.

I crawled toward two girls sharing a hole in a dead tree and tried to squeeze in, but there was no room. I had to hide behind a bush.

The soldiers had finally freed the skiff from the sandbar and were motoring through the bodies, using bayonets to skewer those still alive. One young fisherman escaped by swimming underwater, bullets pocking the sea around him; another dove under the cover of the reef, and a fourth got as far as the mangroves before disappearing into the shadows. Any one of them might have been Philip.

The soldiers landed the boat and fanned out across the beach. They ignored the moaning old men and bayoneted the tall grass instead. They even jabbed at the smoking heap of our house. One of the soldiers stepped toward the jungle and looked directly at me. I held my breath and tried to shrink into the foliage. For a second or two, he appeared to stare right into my face, into the very veins of my tattoos. Then he abruptly about-faced.

Another soldier was shouting. He'd pulled a military boot off a dead elder's foot and was comparing the boot to his own. They looked like a match. He bent down and tore a copper wire off the old man's earlobe, then kicked him in the head to see if he was still alive. When the old man didn't respond, he lanced him with his bayonet just to make sure, then ordered the others to loot the bodies. My soldier trotted back, and, tramping upon the moaning and the dead alike, he and his mates stripped the elders of their talismans.

I looked around for Philip again. The floating dead had bunched together by the sea grass, along with a flotilla of coconut husks. I couldn't tell blond hair from black, short from tall. I couldn't even distinguish a coconut husk from a human head. Suddenly, I began sobbing in silent, racking shudders. I don't believe it was grief yet. I was weeping from gratitude that I could still hope that Philip was among the lucky ones who'd escaped the bullets.

The women muffled their babies and began fleeing into the thick jungle. I ran with them until we reached the muddy banks of the swamp. Hoisting their babies over their heads, they waded into the black water. I was handed a toddler as I entered the ooze. Just as my chin sank under the surface and the child in my arms flailed, just as my foot plunged into the bottomless muck and I felt myself going under, a wooden bridge materialized beneath my feet. Only halfway across did it occur to me that I was stepping on Ishmael's wooden masks and carvings.

On the far side, the mountains began in earnest, rising perpendicularly out of the canopy. We hurried up the slippery footpath, clawing at handholds.

Some five stories high, in a fold of rock above the village, was a narrow passageway that opened onto a massive limestone cavern. In places, the rock was so porous sunlight pierced through.

We all huddled together and listened for the soldiers. The chamber amplified every sound. Even the distant surf reverberated off the walls.

Suddenly, we heard squealing. It sounded human to me,

but Laadah said it was the pigs, that the soldiers must be in the village killing the pigs.

I could feel the hysteria. On the beach, we'd each been crystallized in shock while our men had been slaughtered, but here in the semidarkness, we wailed and wept for the pigs.

No bullets were fired. The soldiers must have been slitting the animals' throats with the bayonets. Each time a pig let out a death squeal, the women cupped their hands over their ears and rocked on their bare knees. I pressed my hands over my ears, too. Only the scent of food stirred me. The soldiers must have torched the yam stores. The vines cloaking the entrance suddenly rustled. The women grabbed their children and buried them beneath their bodies. I balled myself up, too. A fisherboy crawled inside. He was wet, shivering, still wearing his regalia for the whale hunt. One old woman rushed over to him, mashed her brow against his, and touched his face. I recognized the boy. He'd been standing beside Philip when the soldiers fired.

In a voice that sounded, to my ears at least, as shrill as a death squeal, I pleaded to know what had happened to Philip.

The young man turned his head very slowly in my direction. Even in the cave's poor light, I could see an opaque glaze of shell shock dulling both of his eyes.

I sat down again.

We waited until the pinpricks of daylight vanished and the porous rock grew red. Then we waited for outright darkness. No one spoke. Weeping was muffled. No one so much as stirred, save to shift a numb foot or rock a child.

Around midnight, I was sure I heard men shouting to one another in the village, but Laadah said it was only the monkeys.

Just before dawn, two more boys crawled into the cave. Everybody had to touch their faces, rub foreheads with them. Then an old man showed up, his hair wet with blood. He kept assuring us that it wasn't his own, but his wife wouldn't believe him. She made him kneel down and lean against her thighs while she parted his hair, fastidiously scrutinizing his scalp as if she were scouring for lice rather than open gashes. Later, eight fishermen arrived. They'd been caught down-current when the shots had been fired. They were besieged with questions.

I kept waiting for his blond head to emerge through the opening. Each time a new arrival crawled in and it wasn't him, I found myself glaring at his rejoicing family with something like hatred.

Finally, someone called to us from the swamp below. He shouted that the soldiers were gone, that the whale had left. Even from five stories high, I knew it wasn't Philip's shout.

I forced my way out into the light with the others. The sky was colorless, the sun gray, the air thick with ash. I could smell the carnage before I saw it. When I finally reached the beach, others dropped to their knees and whimpered, but I walked right up to Philip.

He was in the shallows with a dozen other bodies, his left foot trapped between two rocks. When the tide drained backward, all the bodies floated with it. When it surged forward again, they all came back. Anchored to the rocks, Philip never strayed. He lay under about a foot of water, faceup. I knelt down beside him. His eyes were open. One minute, the frothy sea would rush into them and turn them milky. The next, it would ebb away and his eyes would become alive under the glimmering water. The bullet had entered his throat just above the ship, where his clavicle bone joined his rib cage. The hole itself was black-edged and bloodless: it looked as though it might have been tattooed on.

Other women began wading into the shallows, too, searching for their husbands and sons. When they caught hold of a body, they grasped it under its arms and dragged it ashore, or if it was only a skinny boy, they bore him in their arms. They must have lined up over two dozen wet shapes on the beach.

The fishermen finally came for Philip, but I wouldn't let them take him. I held him tightly around his chest. One of the men reached down and lifted the rock pinning Philip's foot. I could feel the ocean immediately start to pull him away from me. A fisherman caught hold of his arms and helped me drag Philip up past the waterline. I made them stop right there. I knew where they would take him and I didn't want Philip in that line. That line looked so permanent.

I sat down beside him. The sun was merciless. It highlighted the dead strips of skin, the waterlogged flesh, the marbled eyes. No more pretending for me that he might cough and miraculously come alive.

The fishermen returned to their own dead. They draped the bodies over their shoulders and staggered into the jungle. The women staggered, too, drunk with grief.

We were finally alone on the beach.

I couldn't quite get myself to look at Philip, yet I couldn't quite look away. He was lying on his back, his neck twisted, his limbs queerly posed. The six black bars covering his face were the most familiar thing about him.

For what remained of the day, I kept vigil over him, shooing away the gulls, picking off the scout ants, chasing away a hungry pig who'd escaped the massacre. When night fell, the giant coconut crabs came out and scuttled toward him in the moonlight, their claws opening and closing like pinking shears. I'd flatten them with rocks, then return to my Philip and brush away more scout ants. At some point, I fell asleep because the next thing I knew, it was dawn and the ants had returned with their armies.

Around noon, the villagers came back to the beach, shouldering their dead. They ferried them in crude bark canoes. They'd even made one for Philip. It had to be for Philip: it was so much longer than the rest. After setting the boats down at the sea's edge, the pallbearers tottered from fatigue, while an old woman broke away from her daughters and tried to climb into a coffin. Mostly, though, people wept into their tattooed hands, or stood swaying, blinking at the dead. In the wet, unstable sand, a couple of the canoes had tipped over on their sides. I could see the bodies inside. They'd been wrapped in banana-leaf shrouds, but the leaves didn't cover everything. I saw what they had done to the bodies. They'd rubbed off the skin.

Laadah came over and sat beside me, running her hand lightly over Philip. She ignored the ants, who were now filing into the hole in his chest. She ignored the loose blue-white skin and the blue-black fingernails. She ignored the odor. She straightened out his rigid arms and legs as best she could, then opened the one eyelid that had fallen shut. She spoke to me in Ta'un'uuan, but very slowly, so that I would understand each word. She said that Philip had to leave with the others—right now—or he'd surely get lost, that the current to the next world isn't all that easy to find. She said I should have allowed her to rub off his tattoos last night because the deities have no use for tattooing, but it was too late now, the tide was going out. She motioned for a couple of fisherboys to come get Philip and put him in his canoe: the other coffins were already being launched. She said the body is only temporarily leased to the living: it should be returned in the same unmarked condition that it was lent.

I knelt down at the watermark as the boys cast Philip adrift. When his coffin reached open sea, it spun northward and joined the flotilla of dead.

The women began scratching at their necks with their fingernails until they broke skin. You could see how the pain was giving them comfort, how the blood quieted even the most crazed of them. I would have done anything for that comfort. I dug my nail into my chest—six times, six vertical bars. Tried to gouge myself. I'm a nail biter. I had to finish up with a thorn.

Blood pooled at the base of each bar. I wiped it away with my fingertip. I could see how transient the lines were underneath. In a minute, they would seal closed; in a day, they would only be red marks; in a week, pink shadows; in a month, there wouldn't even be a trace of my Philip.

I rose to my feet, walked over to the charred ruins of our house, knelt, and scoured the cold ashes until I felt something sharp, a shell point or a bone point, I didn't care. I filled a coconut bowl with ash and seawater.

Somebody had to mix the ink.

Somebody had to pick up the needle.

PART THREE

BODY OF WORK

It's one thing to have torn my flesh in the throes of grief, then blackened in the wounds as a reminder, and it's quite another to have spent the next thirty years methodically refashioning myself into a piece of living tapestry. I have inhabited my art for so long with nothing to reflect it back at me. But standing before the vanity mirror in my suite at the Waldorf, naked and alone under the electric lights, I see myself whole for the first time, and only now do I begin to grasp what I had been composing all along.

The effect isn't nearly as grand as I would have liked. The composition lacks a certain spontaneity, the elbows and knees are too symmetrical, and the colors aren't retaining their initial vibrancy. Or maybe they were too subtle to begin with? I should have added more red to that shoulder, and underpainted that foot, the one with my coffin on the bottom of it, in raw umber. And some of the imagery now strikes me as clichéd. The American flag on my right biceps. I wanted it to exude the spirit of a sailor's tattoo. It was meant to be an homage, yet now it looks so cheap and common. It's for the three young marines who came ashore not long after the massacre. They smelled of spearmint gum and American cigarettes. They shared their C rations and chocolate bars with us. Their faces looked so blank to me. When I finally spoke up, my East Side accent coming out of my tattooed lips, their smiles froze. I asked them to tell me everything that had happened since I'd become marooned. They said we were at war, that the Japanese had attacked Pearl Harbor. I didn't know where Pearl Harbor was. I begged them to take me with them. They said it was too dangerous. They promised to send help back for me as soon as the war allowed. A fisherman later told me that he'd heard from another fisherman, who in turn had heard it from a copra trader, that they'd been killed on the island of Tarawa, that all the whites were dead.

Or here on my left elbow is a skull and crossbones, not quite as crudely rendered as a pirate's skull and crossbones, but still. It's for the half-drowned Japanese soldier who washed up on the beach a few months after the marines. We beat him to death with rocks and sticks, then let the birds peck at his flesh until he was only bones. We let the surviving pigs chew on them.

Or here on my right knee, taking up far too much room, are two crosses for the two missionaries from Utah, Jeremiah and Ester, who sailed into the cove a few years after the war. I was so tattooed by that time, they didn't recognize me as one of their own even when I spoke with my unmistakable accent. They had come to Ta'un'uu to preach to the islanders, whom they called the children of Cain, that there wasn't going to be a place for them at heaven's table unless they gave up tattooing. They said good Christians had won the war because they had had God on their side. The islanders asked me to punish them for their lies by engraving their faces. As native as I'd gone by then, I couldn't make myself do it. I let them out of the pig-pen that night and pointed them to the beach. I could have asked them to take me with them. They were sailing to New Guinea to proselytize the Papuans. How would I have gotten home from there? I didn't even know where New Guinea was. And how could I have run away in the night without say-ing goodbye to my friends and neighbors—they'd shared every meal with me for seven years—*and* leave in the company of missionaries? Crosses? Couldn't I have thought of something more original?

Or here on my left clavicle, a lipstick kiss sewn closed with a needle and thread. It now strikes me as one of those high con-cepts that seems so clever at the time but wears out as fast as chalk. It's to mark the third time I might have asked to go home, but didn't. A tiny sloop anchored in our lagoon around my fourteenth or fifteenth year. I'd long ago stopped counting the years. We assembled into our Great Tapestry to welcome the blond man who swam ashore. From a distance, he looked just like a young Philip. He spoke no English and we spoke no Swedish. From what he conveyed with gestures and sand draw-ings, we managed to deduce that he was sailing around the globe, solo. The Ta'un'uuans walked away in disgust. Why would a young man voluntarily sail away from home and leave his parents to grow old alone, then sail right back for no reason whatsoever? The poor Swede didn't know what was going on and started running for his boat. I thought about shouting after him to take me with him, but I wasn't sure any longer where, exactly, home was.

But there are other images, entire friezes of tattoos, where I seem to have outdone myself. The whole left half of my rib cage. If I squint, then block out the right half with my outstretched hand, it's rather brilliant. My fearless use of black has resolved the problem of composing on an aging form. From certain angles, you don't even notice the changes. The lines look like X-rays. Or here on my tongue, my latest tattoo, the firmament. I wanted it to seem like the heavens moved when I spoke. Or here at the base of my throat, the etching for my union boy, a needle engraving a needle, and next to it, a harpoon for my Ta'un'uuan lovers. I took one or two over the years. And here on my lower thigh, the marble arch in Washington Square. I employed a varicose vein to marble in the marble. I wanted the symbol of my youth to age as I aged. Or here on my right earlobe, like a piece of family jewelry, my father's bewildered and terrified face, and on my right, hard as a diamond, my mother's arrogant and terrified face, and in the middle, life-sized, their daughter's ravaged one.

I can now see the differences between Ishmael's art and my own. Where he composed spontaneously, letting his spirit dictate the line, I designed my imagery beforehand and commissioned a helper to engrave it on me. My lines, though competent, can never compare with his virtuosity. But there is something to be said for my process over his. I had to calculate into the design of each tattoo not only the skill level of my helper but also my own ability to withstand the pain of every additional layer of color, of every extraneous detail, of every act of unnecessary bravado. The greatness of the tattoo artist lies in her ability to gauge the degree to which she can push her art before the art kills the canvas.

There were many days, especially during those first years, when I'd brace myself for the prick of the needle, wondering if

I'd gone mad on this piece of rock. Why did I keep inflicting my art on myself? What did it matter? But, invariably, the questions would segue into . . . Is this line too thick? Is that one too thin? Does this image say what I want it to say? Is that one too common? And who will let me know if it is? Who will be my critic? Who will be my audience? Who will be my champion? Who will love me?

Philip's loss in those moments was so chilling that I'd start to shiver under the equatorial sun. Then I would stop working, stop sleeping, stop eating.

One by one they came to me while I was in these trances of grief, imploring me to tattoo them. Whether it was because they so admired my work or because they were willing to sacrifice themselves to pull me back to life, I didn't know. My first commission came from Ishmael's widow. She wanted me to engrave a death mask of her husband on her left breast, as I had engraved a death mask of Philip on mine. Her skin, particularly near the neck, was so scarred from grieving, so crosshatched with inked reminders, that I wasn't sure if my line would be visible. I mixed an opaque white with palm sap and pulverized seashells, mother-of-pearl, so that the pigment would refract sunlight. It took me three weeks of experimentation to find just the right thickness. It took me another month to etch the death mask with all its tattoos. When I finally finished, and the salves were peeled off, she looked down at the portrait on her breast, a photographic negative of Ishmael's face, and pressed her forehead against mine. She said she didn't know tattoos could be made out of light.

My next commission was for a fisherboy. He wanted an iron nail engraved on his body so that he might have better luck finding a real one. He said if he had an iron nail of his own, he could make an iron hook to catch enough fish to get married. I mixed a pale neutral gray, a shade that is only visible in bright daylight, and tattooed a penny nail on his palm. I wanted the nail to appear anew every morning, like the miracle of stigmata. If my tattoo wasn't really magic, at least it would remind him to keep looking for that nail.

Then there was the commission for Laadah, my dear Laadah—now dead twenty years—who marched us to the taro fields during those first months of despair, and made us plant for the future. On her I drew a garden that never needed tending.

And there were so many others. Shy girls who would whisper to me the names of their secret lovers so that I might encode them on their flesh; and the very old, with so little virgin skin left, and so much still to say. It was endless. Someone would die, then a baby would be born, then a fisherman lost his arm to a shark, and his tattoos had to be moved onto his brother's arm before any fishing could resume. And there were always the carefree young men and women, born after the massacre, who thought every one of their exploits deserved a tattoo. They had no idea how finite the body is. One day, as I was about to initiate a bride-to-be, her first tattoo, her whole life yet to be written, I happened to glance down at my drawing hand. It was poised above her pristine abdomen, needle at the ready. My hand looked so frail, the skin so thin, the tattoos so faded. My fingers weren't exactly shaking, but I noticed a tremor in the needle's shaft. I'd become an old woman here.

One of my duties as a tattoo artist is to sing as I insert the needle and ease the suffering with melody. The prayer the Ta'un'uuans traditionally sing tells the story of the first tattoo artist, a young chief who had boundless strength, great talent as a carver, enough wooden matches to light enough fires to warm himself and his people for a thousand years, an enormous penis, one hundred beautiful *and* appreciative wives, and many healthy children, but no wisdom. One day, he left his life of bounty and paddled his canoe to where this world met the next. There he asked his ancestors to reward him for the journey by revealing all their secrets to him. His ancestors didn't respond. So he cut off the tip of his finger and used the spurting blood to paint animals and plants and suns and stars on his flesh, then insisted his ancestors reward him for his ingenuity and talent. The dead sent rain to wash away his offering. Using the fishhook he'd brought along to feed himself, he carved all the animals and plants and sun and stars right into his flesh, then implored his ancestors to reward him for his suffering. The dead only stopped the bleeding, and the wounds sealed shut, and the scars disappeared, and still he possessed no wisdom. So he burned his canoe, then mixed the ash with seawater to make ink, and opened up all his wounds again, and tattooed himself. The dead weren't impressed. Finally, he was a very old man without a canoe, treading water in the middle of the ocean. He asked the dead to take pity on him and let him onto their shore so he might rest. No shore appeared. So he peeled off his skin and threw it into the sea and as he sank, as the dead finally pulled him into their world, he saw the fishes and squids and gulls tear apart his art, all his hard work, and eat the pieces of skin, and that's when he gleaned what the dead had to teach him.

To sing the Ta'un'uuan tattoo prayer as it should be sung, in its entirety, every verse a week-long chant, I would have had to have started memorizing it in childhood.

Instead, each time I inserted the needle, I sang the only songs I remembered, the ones my father had sung to me about the storybook *yeshiva* on the windy Russian steppes, or the little union girl who takes on the bosses. When even those simple lyrics escaped me, I chanted the Hebrew prayers I'd committed to memory under the threat of the rabbi's rod in the dank *cheders* of the Lower East Side. I sang about a people lost in a desert searching for home for forty years. If the Ta'un'uuans didn't know what a desert was, surely they knew what it was to be alone in the middle of an unbroken horizon.

About four months ago, a seaplane landed in our lagoon. We'd seen planes before, certainly during the war, or nowadays the high white streaks of jets crossing the Pacific, or the twin-engine Pipers of the missionaries who proselytize to the north of here. We hurried to the beach to assemble into the Great Tapestry. My place is now on the far left, third from the end, among the elders. The right half is made up of fisher-boys and young marrieds, their tattooed bodies so bright and taut, whereas we on our end look like the fraying fringe of an old flag.

A white man, necklaced with cameras, and a white woman, sporting what looked like an old-fashioned bathing costume (capris, I later learned), stepped onto the wing and waved to us. They wore the same expressions of astonishment, I imagine, that Philip and I had worn when we first saw the Great Tapestry.

The man lifted a camera and aimed it at us, while the

woman slipped out of her red sandals, eased herself off the wing, stepped into the water, and waded toward the beach. When she got to the rocks, she put her sandals back on, stepped onto the pink sand, then shielded her eyes from the dizzying sun with a bare blond arm and asked for me by name. A sudden wind gust tore the chiffon kerchief off her hair, and she reeled around to catch it.

I hadn't heard my full name in nearly three decades.

After securing the pink kerchief with a double knot under her chin, she hooded her eyes once again, with a hand this time, and swept her gaze over the tapestry, as you might inspect an unfurled bolt of silk for a snag.

"Mrs. Ehrenreich? Sara Ehrenreich?" she asked again, all the while searching our faces, one after the other, all the way down the line. "I've brought news of home and a few mementos that might interest you." She opened a purse slung from her shoulder and took out what looked like a couple of photographs. "I've also brought gifts for the Ta'un'uuans." She waved to the photographer. He lowered his camera just long enough to unlatch the cargo hatch near the plane's tail.

I could make out bright-colored boxes in the dark underbelly. I couldn't see what the packages contained, but I certainly recognized the palette of the modern world.

She smiled at the fisherboys and they shyly smiled back. "If one of you gentlemen will volunteer his canoe, we can bring the gifts ashore right now."

The right half of the tapestry was quaking to come undone and see what the whites had brought them. I could almost feel sparks running down the line of young bodies, whereas on my end, the faded fringe, we watched with deep skepticism.

One of the fisherboys couldn't hold himself back any longer.

He sprinted for his canoe. Then the whole right side began coming apart. It advanced toward the woman, encircling her. She looked as if she were being rolled up in a Persian rug. Easing herself free of the fisherboys and young mothers, she approached us elders, two old men and twelve old ladies, one of them me.

"I'm from *Life* magazine. You must remember *Life,* Mrs. Ehrenreich." Her eyes never stopped scanning our old tattooed visages for something recognizable. She shuffled through her two photographs, picked one out, then held it up for each of us to study. The picture was taken at my debut exhibit at Gloria Vanderbilt Whitney's salon. Philip and I posed in the main gallery. I recognized Philip's hobnail boots and my boa, though our faces were somewhat out of focus. I also recognized the drawing of my *davening* father behind us, *City of Coffins.* "What makes you think she's still alive?" I asked. I've never lost my accent.

A faint smile played at the corners of the young woman's coral lips as she studied my face again, couldn't take her eyes off it. Her own expression was a mix of fascination and revulsion. Untattooed faces are so easy to read.

"The scientists aboard the USS *Neptune* told us."

A steel boat, about the size of a tugboat, had anchored offshore during our last dry season. The men on board had offered to trade us their cigarette lighters for fresh fruit and water. We then offered to trade our carvings for tobacco and canned fruit. They told us they were astronomers, men who study the heavens, and that they'd come to our island to witness a total eclipse of the sun. They explained what a total eclipse of the sun was, demonstrating with three coconuts. The Ta'un'uuans knew perfectly well what a solar eclipse was. It's a shadow cast by the world of the dead on the world of the living. The scientists invited all the youngsters on board to look through their giant telescope. That night, I paddled out in a canoe, and I asked if I might look, too. The men were topside, sharing a bottle of Courvoisier. A bearded one helped me up the rope ladder and offered me a sip from his glass. He called me "auntie" and asked where I'd learned my excellent English. I told him at a missionary school. The cognac smelled medicinal and achingly familiar. I took a sip, then another, until I polished off the whole glass. I held it out for a refill. He exchanged looks with the others, then politely replenished my drink. On my fourth cognac, he jokingly asked, "Where did a nice old auntie like you learn to drink like that?"

"At the Savoy. Though I prefer Hennessy," I said. The man's expression was no less flabbergasted than if, say, the ship's cat had quipped up that she preferred one brand of tuna over another. When the scientists finally recovered from their shock, they plied me with questions. The cognac had taken effect: I vaguely remember answering one or two. Then I asked to see the stars. They led me to the prow of the ship and sat me beside the giant telescope. A redhead showed me how to focus the eyepiece. I placed my eye against the cold glass. I could no more comprehend that I was witnessing the staggering beauty of the stars in close-up than I could accept that the sweet aftertaste on my tongue was really cognac. That's when I got the inspiration to engrave the firmament on my tongue's tip.

"The scientists said they'd met you last year, Mrs. Ehrenreich," the young woman said.

I took the picture of Philip and me out of her hand and

examined it closely—the yellowing paper, the frayed edge, the scratches. Philip was a tall blur with a white mane, and my boa was in sharper focus than my face, but I could make out every line in my drawing, every decision, every mistake.

"I've got others. All sorts of documents. Would you like to see them, Sara?"

"Where did you get this?"

"Do you mind if I call you Sara? I searched old archives. Rumors of your existence have circulated for years. Soldiers from the Second World War claimed they'd met a stranded American woman on a South Pacific island. There was even talk of you and Amelia Earhart being one and the same."

She started to show me an old newspaper clipping, but I looked away. I wasn't sure I wanted to see it.

The fisherboy had just finished loading the gifts into his canoe and was now paddling ashore. The photographer was crouching on the prow, taking pictures. By the time they reached land, the tapestry was in such tatters anyway that the elders abandoned their places to see what the canoe contained. I turned to join them.

"We just want to talk to you, Sara," she shouted after me. "I've brought lots of pictures. I've brought copies of *Life* dating back to the year you disappeared. Men have walked on the moon. We've cured polio. Movies are in color. Aren't you curious?"

The youngsters were holding themselves back until I joined the other elders for the blessing of the cargo, a row of boxes on the beach. The chief's first wife, Laadah's oldest daughter, picked up a small one and held it toward the sun, trying to see if the container was transparent enough for her to peer through the designs and see what was inside. She motioned for me to take counsel with her. She whispered that no one on Ta'un'uu had ever before seen the hard shell that the cargo gestated in. She was surprised to find that it was tattooed. She asked me if the shells themselves were the gifts, or if there was something more inside. I didn't recognize any of the products pictured on the boxes. I didn't recognize the trademarks emblazoned across the cardboard. I no longer recognized the words. Maybe it had been too many years. Or maybe a whole other language had been invented during my absence.

When the boxes were finally opened, the contents disappointed the islanders. Though the younger set found ways to use the wristwatches (the men wore them at the base of their penis gourds), the elders had no use for the walkie-talkies, or the bicycle, or the gadgetry I could no longer name. The steak knives, however, were prized by everyone. While the youngsters examined the cargo, the elders studied the broken shells. They remarked on the beauty of the shells' colors, the precision of the tattooing, the simplicity of the designs, then tried to piece them back together again. They carefully aligned halved flaps that had been torn open in haste by the youngsters, then sealed shut the wounds with tree gum.

When the boxes were whole again, they called for their children to carry the beautiful shells to the village and hang them up in the meetinghouse next to the carvings.

I was sitting in front of my own shell, a plain cardboard box of old *Life* magazines, and a second photograph of Philip and me. The reporter was seated across from me, her photographer fifty feet away, as if to give me my privacy, but I recognized a telephoto lens.

"We couldn't carry the whole library, Sara. There were more than fifteen hundred magazines. We brought mostly covers, as you can see, but I did go through the stacks to select a few issues I thought might interest you."

I picked up the second photograph: Philip and me marching down Fifth Avenue, our mouths open in song, our fists raised, our stride so confident. It almost looks as if our side had won. It was taken during the Rockefeller protest. I recognized the placards. But when I looked more closely at Philip—I couldn't tear my eyes off him—I noticed white dust from the plaster ruins of Rivera's mural on his threadbare overcoat and a cast of exhaustion in his eyes.

"I found them in the archive at the Museum of Modern Art. Did you know the museum has one of your paintings hanging in its collection?" She checked her notes. "*Self-Portrait Without Vanishing Point,* 1923."

So they prefer my early work.

I put the photograph back in the box, under the magazines. I had no intention of weathering the deluge of memories that image was about to unleash with that camera pointed at my face. When the reporter saw her photographer wasn't going to get a picture of the old castaway breaking down, she lifted out one of the magazines and placed it in my hands.

"We thought it might be easier on you to begin at the beginning. Isn't that the month you and Philip disappeared?"

Rosalind Russell was on the cover. The price was 10 cents. The date read September 4, 1939.

"I found records of your passage, old copies of Philip's and your passport applications, a bank draft in Philip's name from the Swiss banker, Richter. Weren't you traveling on a Japanese ocean liner?"

I lifted out a handful of covers and caught the scent of old paper. I hadn't smelled that particular must in so long. I laid them in my lap. They were very fragile. The paper had aged even faster than my skin. Gingerly, I begin leafing through them. A tiny submarine. *German U-boat,* the title read. *Mussolini. Summer Fashions. The Military Look. Claudette Colbert* in a sailor cap. I turned over *Claudette Colbert.* A Viceroy cigarette ad was on the back. It featured a tuxedoed man and a woman in furs smoking Viceroys in a hansom cab on Fifth Avenue. For a moment, this silly ad almost unleashed what the photograph of Philip and me hadn't, but I held myself in check.

"How did you end up here, Sara? Why did you stay?"

Betty Grable. Skating Fashions for Winter. Kids' Football. German Plane. French Sentry.

"When did the war begin?" I asked.

"For us?" She leaned over the box and grabbed another handful of images. She hadn't even been born. The war was ancient history to her. I noticed this stack included pages. An American flag was on the top cover. The caption read, *U.S. Goes to War.* The date, *December 10, 1941.*

One by one the elders came over to see what my shell contained. They squatted behind me at a respectful distance, peering over my shoulder, careful not to let their shadows be cast on the images. It was impolite for someone's shadow to darken a tattoo before it was completely healed, and they didn't know how fresh these images were.

Sunken Battleships. Nursing Shortage. Coastal Defense. U.S. Warplanes. USO Singer. Barrage Balloons. Ginger Rogers.

When the elders saw that the ink wasn't coming off on my

hands, that there was no blood on my fingertips, they moved closer and formed a half circle around me, picking through the magazine covers themselves, careful not to tear the friable paper. They didn't know there was an order to the covers, and even if I'd told them, I'm not sure Western dates would have made much sense to them. Besides, they weren't interested in the latest movie star, they were studying images of the war. *Torpedoed Ship. War Glider. Soldier in the Snow. Captured Nazis.* Bombs exploding. A soldier making a victory sign in front of a giant marble swastika. And photographs of skeletons. Skeletons staring through barbwire. Skeletons looking out from dark shelves. Skeletons watching the machinations of the living with dazed, sunken eyes. A burly American soldier, spade in hand, kneeling before an enormous pit of charred human remains that he and his unit had just unearthed.

The elders asked me whose death was being avenged, and why did so many lives need to be sacrificed for it? And who would treat the human dead like this? And how did the bones at the bottom of the pile make it to the sanctuary of their ancestors? Is this the world you come from, Sara?

One by one, they pressed their foreheads against mine and walked back to the village, leaving me alone with my dead. A Ta'un'uuan never wants to be alone, especially in times of grief, but they knew me so well.

The reporter placed her hand lightly on mine. "You don't have to go through them all now," she said. "They're yours to keep, Sara. You must have so many questions. You must feel so . . . *overwhelmed.*"

I wasn't sure what I was experiencing at that moment, but I certainly didn't want this young lady with her blank, unmarked face to name it for me.

When she finally realized I wasn't going to confide in her, she patted my hand again, then signaled her photographer to stop shooting and slowly backed away.

MacArthur in Japan. Welcome Home, Navy. When had the war ended? Couldn't someone have come for me then? Winston Churchill, cigar in mouth, paintbrush in hand. He took up painting? *Hope and Crosby. Party Season. Spring Fashions. Homesteads for Vets. Occupied Germany. Co-ed Clothes. The Russian People. Summer Hats. Broadway Beauties. Palestine.* An Arab on a camel, no sight of a Zionist. *Greta Garbo. Mid-Century Issue. Spring Fashions.* The hems are going up. Another and another pretty face. I must have crossed the date where the movie stars were still recognizable to me. *Natural Childbirth. Winter Hats. Atomic War.* A colossal waterspout mushrooming over the ocean. *Ice Skating Beauties. Best Bird Dogs. Astro Chimp,* a monkey in a space suit. *Citizen Ike. Alan Shepard,* a man in a space suit. Clark Gable, looking so old, in a cowboy hat. But at least I recognized him. *Princess Margaret's Wedding. Trampoliners. Alaska's Animals. Soviet Race to Space. Cancer Surgeon. Pope John XXIII.* Battleships—or are they cargo ships?—on a horizon. *Cuban Missile Crisis. China Invades India.* More pretty faces. *Ann-Margret. Jean Seberg. The Beauty of Food. Sid Caesar in* Little Me. *Nelson and Happy Rockefeller. Special Issue: A Long Visit with the Soviet People. Special Issue: 16 Pages of Fantastic Color: The Space Walk.* I turned the page, so curious to see the pictures, but the reporter had failed to select it as an issue that "might" interest me. *Navy Patrol in the Mekong Delta. China's Red Guards. Bathing Suits in Fashion at Acapulco. Elizabeth Taylor. Leonardo da Vinci Sketch. U.S. Paratroopers in Vietnam. Montreal's Expo '67. Mia Farrow. Israeli Soldier Cools Off in the Suez Canal. Remembering Stalin. Human Heart Recipient. Spe-*

cial Issue: Moon Walk. A flag and footprints in what looked to me like a desert. *Spring Fashions.* And the last one, *Ballet Dancer.* November 3, 1969. 40 cents. I did the arithmetic. Thirty years, two months, and eight days.

I left the covers where they lay strewn on the beach, picked up the photographs of Philip and me, and started for home. My house is one of the oldest stilt structures in the village. The huts are arranged in concentric circles, and mine is in the inner ring. I climbed the ladder, crawled under the low straw doorway, sat in a patch of daylight, and studied the photographs again. Philip was still leading the procession, hair flying. I was at his elbow. He looked so brazen and so broken. I ran the pad of my fingertip over his hair, his throat, his chest, his mouth open in song. Try as I did, I couldn't remember what his voice sounded like, and this, above all else, is what finally undid me.

An hour or so later, the reporter and the photographer stood at the foot of my ladder. "Sara, are you up there?" she called. "A fisherman was kind enough to show us where you live."

I heard her mount the bottom rung.

"I have another photograph, a gift from an old friend of yours."

She continued climbing the rungs until her kerchiefed head cleared the balcony. I was seated under the straw eaves on my only chair, a bamboo rocker. She held out the picture and I took it. This one showed a wall of my paintings hung salon-style.

"Alice Bronsky, Julien's widow, wanted you to have it if I should ever find you. She spoke so fondly of you and Philip. May I come up? I'm not used to ladders."

I offered her my hand and she nervously ascended the last rungs in her red sandals. She crawled away from the ledge. "I never introduced myself. Brooke. Brooke Wilson. And that's Jack," she said. Jack waited at the foot of the ladder, changing lenses.

"When did Julien die?" I asked.

She reached back into her purse, took out her notebook and a kind of pen I'd never seen before (ballpoint, I later learned). "Nineteen fifty-two. Alice told me how he never stopped championing your work." She reached out and patted my hand once again. The touch was clumsy and officious compared to a Ta'un'uuan's. "You must have many other questions, Sara. I'll try to answer what I can."

Her face assumed an expression so earnest and uninformed that I doubt that blank oval could have answered any questions I had.

"We don't have to talk about the past," she said finally. She looked around at my scant possessions—the bamboo rocker, the mats, the cooking pots, and my inks and needles. She picked up a six-inch ivory one adorned with figurines. "It's beautiful," she said. "Is it used for weaving?"

"It's a tattoo needle."

She quickly put it down, practically dropped it, then lifted a corner of a mat and pretended to admire the weaving, but I saw her eyes make quick forays back to my needles—bamboo, turtle shell, pig tusk, wood, iron, and a human bone for the deep punctures.

Her eyes returned to my face, then strayed down to my old, flaccid left breast. "It's a portrait of Philip, isn't it?"

I looked down at the faded tattoo. I spent half my life trying to live with him, and the other half trying to live without him.

"May I invite Jack to come up here?" she asked. "May we take some pictures?" I could see that mix of fascination and revulsion return to her guileless face. "Your tattoos are extraordinary. I've never seen anything like them. Others should see them, too. Wouldn't you like us to photograph them for posterity?"

I knew that to her I was but a cross between Mrs. Crusoe, a shipwrecked Gauguin, and a sideshow freak—*Tattooed White Lady Artist Found Among Savages.* But my tattoos *are* my very finest work, the closest I'll ever come to genius. As native as I'd become, I still clung to the Western illusion that if my art was any good, it would enter the ranks of art history and outlast my mortal body.

I hadn't yet learned what the dead had to teach me.

I agreed to be photographed.

That evening, the villagers graciously prepared a feast for our guests on the beach. We sacrificed one of our most beloved sows, and sang about her many accomplishments, her twenty-six children, fifty grandchildren, and ninety-eight great-grandchildren. Then we roasted her body and ate it.

The children kept dashing up to Jack, trying to get his camera to focus on them. They had no idea what a camera did, let alone what a lens was, but they intuited that if they curried favor from that cyclopean eye, it might bestow power on them.

The feast lasted all night. The sow was over three hundred pounds. When the sun finally crested the treetops, Brooke asked, "Do you think they might line up again for us, Sara, the way they did when we landed?" She smiled at the chief and his brother to my right, at the eleven old ladies to my left. "It was glorious to see the full display yesterday. May we take some more pictures?"

The elders took counsel among themselves, then turned to me. "We understand what the camera does, Sara, that the whites have found a way to acquire tattoos without suffering the pain on their own skin. Should we let them own our likenesses with no sacrifice on their part?"

The youngsters must have overheard Brooke's request to form the Great Tapestry because they were already taking their places in the grand design. I would be a liar not to confess how much I wanted *all* of my art properly documented for posterity. After all, I'd been working on the Tapestry for thirty years.

I rose to my feet and the whole left fringe followed.

When they finally got their pictures, Brooke asked me to join her for a stroll along the shore.

She opened her purse and took out a pack of cigarettes. Chesterfields. My old brand. She offered me one, then lit one for herself. "Thanks for your help back there," she said in a conspiratorial whisper of blue smoke. "We wouldn't have gotten the shots without you."

She waited until the last of the villagers were out of earshot, then reached back into her purse for a white envelope. "They're the only personal effects of yours I could find, aside from the photographs. There's a letter of yours to Julien and Alice, copies of your old art reviews. I also put in a manifesto that Philip wrote and you signed in 1922. Alice gave them to me. I thought you might want them."

I took the envelope, but I didn't open it.

"We don't have to talk about your past, Sara. I understand. We can talk about the here and now. I'll write only what you want me to." She reached for her notebook and pen.

"May I see that?" I asked, pointing to the pen. I held it up to the sun. A single blue vein ran the length of its shaft. I lightly jabbed the metal nib against my fingertip. It was too dull for penetration. I asked for a piece of paper, then ran the point across it—fluent, effortless, very fast, but so unvarying, so passionless.

I returned the pen, but I asked if I could have the Chesterfields.

"We're leaving at noon. A storm's coming. Jack waded out to the plane last night and checked the radio. It's going to last for days. We have to get back. We're on a deadline." She glanced at the darkening horizon, then threw down her cigarette and crushed it with the toe of her sandal. It still had a good inch of tobacco left. She suddenly reeled around and took my hand once again, sandwiched it between hers. "Why don't you come back to New York with us, Sara?"

The pivot was so calculated, the touch so synthetic. She must have planned this all along. *Tattooed White Lady Artist Found Among Savages* doesn't sell as many magazines as *Tattooed White Lady Artist Found Among Savages Comes Home After Thirty Years: 16 Pages of Fantastic Color.* Why had she waited until the last hour to ask me? Did she think I could just drop everything here at a moment's notice?

"It doesn't mean forever. Two, three weeks. *Life* will pay all expenses. Aren't you curious to see what's become of your world?"

"Curious" didn't even share the same synonyms with what I felt.

"You'll be in New York City by tomorrow night."

Less time than it takes to paddle to the next island.

"Don't you want to see your home again?"

I tried to imagine standing on a New York street corner, flagging down a taxi. The last *Life* cover had read November. It was late autumn. If the idea astounded me, it also saddened me, as if going home after all these years was just another variation on grief.

I withdrew my hand.

"Please promise me you'll think about it, Sara. We won't be leaving for another hour or so."

As if I would think about anything else. She walked back to the feast site. I finished my cigarette. There would be smoke shops on every block. Matches free for the taking. How many other chances would I have to go home at my age?

Brooke started folding up tripods, collecting the bags. Jack was taking some last shots of the elders. The chief and his brother were fashioning a bark coffin. Laadah's daughter and the women scoured the cold fire pit for the sow's bones.

Who besides Alice Bronsky would remember me? Who was still alive? After three decades, what could two weeks possibly reveal? The latest fashions? The newest ism?

Laadah's daughter called me to help them prepare the sow for the next world. The elders were now arranging the charred bones in the bark coffin. Thunderheads were piling up over the cliffs. The surf was growing wilder. The plane tugged on its anchor. Soon the sea would be too rough for it to take off, let alone for the elders to launch the coffin.

The elders lifted up the bark canoe and ferried it toward the shoreline. The tide was coming in fast. Laadah's daughter called for my help again.

Brooke and Jack conferred. He started wading out to the plane, while she turned and shouted, "We have to leave right now, Sara."

A breaker exploded against the cliff. Another crested the reef. Brooke came up behind me. "We can't wait any longer, we won't be able to take off. Are you coming?"

The elders wouldn't launch the coffin without me. If the coffin didn't start out right now, the sow's bones would never clear the reef. They'd be left to drift back and forth with the tide for all eternity. I walked to the water's edge and picked up my share of the coffin.

The moment the plane took off, I experienced profound relief, then growing apprehension, then dire longing for what I had so impulsively turned down. After all, I could have insisted that Brooke ignore her deadline and wait out the storm for me. Over the next few days, I consoled myself that my art could speak for itself, that it didn't matter if my mortal body had chosen to remain here. But then an ache for home I thought I'd long ago extinguished would rage over me like a fever.

The elders became concerned. They may not have understood what homesickness was, but they certainly recognized loss. They sent their best paddler, Laadah's great-nephew, north to another island where their distant cousins lived with a white missionary couple. The fishermen said the missionaries had a machine that could talk to the afterworld, that they would know how to beckon the seaplane back for me.

The paddler returned four days later with a note from the missionaries. They had reached a ham radio operator in Salt Lake City who, in turn, promised to relay the message on to *Life*.

Life returned a second time, as soon as the typhoon season had ended. The plane touched down in our cove again, but no one turned off the propellers. They'd brought a rubber dinghy this time. I was standing in my place at the far left of the Tapestry, holding a small packed satchel. I have so few possessions of any importance, except, of course, my skin.

When the dinghy came ashore, Brooke and Jack didn't climb out. Brooke shouted to the islanders over the roar of the engine, "We can't stay and visit this time, but we'll be back soon. With gifts." She motioned me to hurry aboard. "There's just enough daylight left to make it back to Port Moresby, Sara."

I stepped away from the others. Laadah's daughter kept hold of my hand, but eventually let me go. I climbed into the dinghy. Jack offered his arm to steady me, as if I hadn't been climbing in and out of dugouts for thirty years.

We approached the airplane from the rear, needles of salt spray stinging our eyes. The cabin wasn't much bigger than an automobile's. Brooke helped me into a jump seat behind her, then strapped me in. I looked back at the beach through my tiny oval window. Beads of seawater ran sideways across the scratched glass. The Tapestry leaned into the man-made wind and hurried forward to the water's edge. I hadn't seen my composition in its entirety since I'd become a part of it. A panel was plainly missing from the far left, but my absence hardly marred the grand design.

The youngsters tried to spot me in one of the plane's four windows. I waved, but they couldn't see me through the spray. Then the far-left fringe of the Tapestry knelt down in the shallows and clawed at their necks with their fingernails. I hammered on the window to try to get them to stop. I shouted that I'd be back before the full moon. But no matter how many times I had told them I'd return, they still believed that I was leaving for the afterworld.

And, perhaps, I was.

PART FOUR

ON DISPLAY

limousine awaited us at LaGuardia Airport. *Life* had booked me first-class all the way from Port Moresby. A chauffeur stood at the bottom of the plane's steel staircase, holding out a fur coat for me. (On loan, I later learned, from Saks.) The temperature was near freezing. I saw my own breath for the first time in decades. For a Ta'un'uuan that's tantamount to seeing one's own soul. Brooke helped me on with the coat, then hurried me into the warm car. She eased herself in beside me, while Jack sat on the jump seat opposite us and reloaded his camera.

We'd been traveling for thirty-six hours. It was 5:30 a.m. by the limousine's clock. The chauffeur backed us away from the plane, then veered off the tarmac. The airport was practically empty, save for an occasional taxi. The model had changed, but I'd recognize that yellow anywhere.

"You ready to see New York again?" Brooke asked.

The limousine windows were so dark I could barely see out. "How do I raise and lower my window?" They'd done away with crank handles.

She reached over and pressed a silver button on my armrest

to demonstrate. The glass fell and rose, fell and rose. We were now speeding past the airport's vast parking lots, then the row houses of Flushing, then the cemeteries of Queens. The first spokes of sunrise were silhouetting the gravestones. I'd forgotten how big the city of coffins was.

"You want to go straight to the hotel, Sara? Or is there anyplace you'd like to stop first? Are you hungry? Should we get something to eat?"

"Can we take the Brooklyn Bridge into Manhattan?" I asked.

"Why not?" she said, smiling. She signaled the chauffeur, and we branched off the highway onto the great cabled expanse of the Brooklyn Bridge. I could sense her watching me closely, trying to read my expression through my tattoos so that she could accurately record my emotional state upon seeing New York again. But the tattoos Ishmael had engraved on my face simply wouldn't allow for that. Had she only known what to look for, she would have realized that the tattoos Ishmael sentenced me to wear expressed exactly what I felt at that moment—fear, wonder, shame, sadness, rapture, laid one atop another.

Jack focused his lens on my face. I lowered my window and did something I hadn't done before, and haven't done since. I posed for the camera, my tattooed profile against the skyscrapers of Manhattan. It was a picture *I* wanted.

The skyline was red. The Woolworth Building, the Chrysler Building, the Empire State Building were still standing, but the gaps between them had been mortared in with new buildings—taller, wider, devoid of human ornament, covered entirely in mirrors. Giant upended glass coffins for titans.

We came ashore on Water Street. I recognized the fishmarket. Gray herrings and gray mackerels on gray ice. Horns and whistles kept blowing. Geysers of steam erupted from manhole covers. Taxis whizzed by. A tumult of coats, hats, and umbrellas waded in front of our hood. During a break in the human flotsam, we turned onto a great avenue of sludge and ice, and rolled with the current of traffic through downtown's sunless canyons. Men in galoshes and women in pumps were funneling into big black caves of polished stone. A bow-backed man, probably my age, was pushing a hot-dog cart across a gusting square—Chatham, I think. Garbage swirled in the updraft. We were heading for lower Broadway. Nothing had changed, and everything had changed. The tin garbage cans were now plastic. The Hebrew signs had become Chinese. The automobiles looked like cheap rockets in a Buck Rogers movie. There were no more streetcars. I couldn't tell if my eyes were tearing from the frigid wind in my face or from a source I thought had long ago gone dry within me. I pressed the button on my armrest and the smoky glass silently ascended over modernity.

"*Life*'s putting you up at the Waldorf-Astoria," Brooke said.

"The Waldorf?" I couldn't help but smile. Philip and I had protested its being built. "May we go by way of the Lower East Side?"

"We can go and do whatever you want."

I rapped on the chauffeur's partition. "Avenue D, please."

He turned north on Bowery. Ragged men still warmed themselves around trash fires. Along Houston Street, the crooked little tenements were still intact, veined now in new pipes, the roofs thick with aerials. Laundry, albeit of a more colorful variety, still snapped from clotheslines.

On the river side of Avenue D, where the smithies once

lived, grim brick barracklike structures had been erected, all the windows barred: to lock the people in or out, I couldn't tell.

"Washington Square, please," I said. The limousine made a left toward Cooper Union, the same route I had strolled every Saturday night in my Gypsy skirt and red stockings, my shop-girl heart hammering with hope. The marble arch was blanketed with snow. A new fountain had been built. The spout was a spray of ice. On University Place, where the Brevoort once stood, was a Chock full o'Nuts. Or maybe the Brevoort wasn't on University? I couldn't remember. We began rolling north toward Union Square, past the statue of George Washington on his prancing horse, under whose marble hooves Philip and I had marched, chanted, locked arms, raised fists, sung with our comrades for a just paradise on earth. It was now edged by department stores. We veered onto Park Avenue South and sailed toward the maw of Midtown.

"Could we go by way of Fifth Avenue?" I asked.

"We'd have to turn around. I'm afraid it's a one-way street now," Brooke said. She started to alert the driver, but I stopped her. Between two low office buildings, I could see the vaulted, silver cupola of the Chrysler Building, steel eagles perched on steel shoulders, the triangular windows alive with the yellow fire of the sun. It looked like a deity.

A cave opened up where none had been, in the middle of Park Avenue, and we tunneled through the bowels of the city only to emerge again beside Grand Central. The sidewalks were black with umbrellas, the sky full of pigeons.

On the north side of the train station, where Park Avenue fronted the wealthy, a hoarfrosted, wrought-iron, tree-lined divider, the width of a tenement building, appeared. Women in furs walked poodles in wool sweaters on bejeweled leads. From between parked cars, uniformed, white-gloved, whistle-blowing doormen stepped into traffic to summon taxis. Evidently, Philip's and my dream of a Marxist utopia hadn't quite come to fruition.

We pulled up to the Waldorf. It wasn't much shorter than the mountain behind my village. A flashbulb flared, then fizzled away on the far side of my dark window. A rush of wan faces crowded around my door, trying to peer in.

"I'm afraid you'll have to get used to it," Brooke said, lowering her window just wide enough to stick out her hand and wave to the doormen. "You're a celebrity. You were featured in *Life*, Sara. A copy's waiting for you in your suite."

The doormen roped off the small crowd, and I was ushered inside. The concierge introduced himself, then ordered a bellhop to carry my bark satchel for me. I told him it wasn't necessary. The hotel guests, men sitting in wingback chairs, women sipping coffee from china cups, surreptitiously studied my tattoos from over their morning newspapers. They were more disturbing than the gawkers outside.

The concierge escorted me to the front desk, where the manager ceremoniously turned the guest book around and handed me a fountain pen. Jack clicked away. "Would you care to sign the registry, Mrs. Ehrenreich?"

I plied the inky nib to the gilt-edged book and signed my name, so curious to see if my signature had changed after so many years. It was remarkably the same.

"May I show you to your suite now?" the manager asked.

"Please," I said.

He and I waited for an elevator, along with Brooke, Jack,

the bellhop, and a preoccupied gentleman who was so upset his umbrella wouldn't close that he didn't notice a tattooed old lady in the fur coat and bark sandals beside him.

"I don't know about you," Brooke whispered to Jack, "but I can't wait to take a hot bath."

We ascended to the forty-second floor. I was shown my home for the next two weeks—foyer, living room, bedroom. On the coffee table, in a silver bowl, apples, oranges, pears, grapes, and gold-wrapped chocolates formed a centerpiece. An issue of *Life,* evidently featuring me, lay beside the bowl.

"May I show you where everything is," the manager said. He opened the drapes to unveil my Park Avenue view, then pointed out the wet bar, the marble bath, the vast, pillowed bed, the dressing area with its triptych of full-length mirrors, and my three telephones, one on the Queen Anne nightstand beside my bed, one in the bathroom, and one on the foyer wall. There were no rotary dials on any of them.

"If there's anything you need or want, just push zero for the front desk or triple zero for my direct line."

Brooke opened the bedroom closet. A dozen or so dresses, the price tags still on, hung in a row. Shoes in open boxes were lined up below them. Though styles had changed, I recognized the timeless uniform of an old lady. "If they don't fit, we'll get others tomorrow," she said. She opened her purse and gave me a folded piece of paper. "It's Alice Bronsky's number, if you want to call her. Would you like me to stay for a while, Sara, until you're used to everything? Are you hungry?"

The manager quickly handed me the room service menu, a leather-bound tome as thick as a novelette. "If you don't see anything you like on the menu," he said, "we'll make something special for you."

"Or we can send out for anything you want," Brooke added.

I could have asked for beluga caviar and French champagne, or a thick steak and a glass of Hennessy, but ever since we'd passed the fishmarket, I'd been craving herring.

"I'd like a piece of pickled herring," I said. "And a Bermuda onion, and a boiled potato, please."

The bellhop was sent to fetch my order. Twenty minutes later, a cart was rolled in with an assortment of herrings, a Bermuda onion *and* a white onion, and four steaming potatoes on three china plates. There was also an array of pickles and sprigs of parsley.

"Bon appétit," Brooke said.

Shadowing himself against the drapery, Jack tried to get a better angle.

"I'd rather not be photographed while I'm eating, if you don't mind," I said. Then I assured Brooke that I'd be fine, that she had seen to my every need. I thanked her and the manager and the bellhop and said, "I'd like to be alone now."

"We'll see you in a few hours. After you get some rest." Brooke smiled, but I could see how disappointed she was that I wouldn't pose for her picture. She hung the DO NOT DISTURB sign on my door, then shut it behind her.

I looked around the suite, out the window. Manhattan heaved and pulsated below me. The room service cart stood near the sofa. I sat down before it and leaned forward to admire the feast, to feel the steam rising off the potatoes. I eased the white linen napkin from under the silverware, then spread it across my lap. I picked up the fork and dinner knife, patterned with the Waldorf's monogram, then sliced off a morsel of fish, a sliver of Bermuda onion, and a wedge of potato. I carefully speared each item onto my fork, then opened my mouth and bit down. Along with a burst of peppercorn, sweet wine, and onion, the taste released a spark or two of memory. Nothing specific. Just palatable déjà vu. But the second bite unleashed a tenderness of such visceral urgency that it almost seemed hallucinatory. To whom was this tenderness directed?

The peppercorn and acidic wine were boring down inside me. They had to bore very far down to actually find me. They had to bore past my years on Ta'un'uu, past my years with Philip, past my shopgirl ambitions, until they reached my parents' kitchen table, on which a plate of pickled herring, a Bermuda onion, and a steaming potato are set in the feeble light of an air shaft window.

I lifted my head. The light was funerary gray. On the far side of a glass opening in the face of a concrete mountain, snow was falling. The dark windows reflected nothing but me in a strange room, on a strange sofa. The clock on the end table read 6:05. Morning or evening, I couldn't say. All three phones were ringing at once. I picked up the closest one. "Hello? Hello?"

"Did you have a good rest, Sara?" Brooke asked. "Do you see the snow? It's your first evening back. Any particular place you'd like to go?"

When I failed to name a single place, she said, "Anyone other than Alice you'd like me to get a phone number for? Anyone you'd like me to call tonight to let them know that you're here? Back?"

I said I wasn't yet sure where I was, that I would see her in the morning. I set the receiver back in its plastic cradle and crossed the carpet. I turned on the bathroom light, then quickly shut it again. I wasn't yet ready to see my life's work reflected back at me. I filled the tub and bathed by moonlight or street-light, I couldn't tell which through the curtains. I found a robe and slippers and stood by the living room window, my wet hand starfished against the glass, over the city's tireless glow. There was no moon, no stars, no planets, no sense of eternity. How had I lived here? How had I not?

I went to the closet, intending to get dressed and go out alone. Uptown, downtown, it didn't matter. I would just keep walking. After all, it wasn't yet seven in the evening. New York was only now coming alive. In my old bohemian life, Philip and I might just be waking up.

The dresses looked like hanging skins. I tried to imagine myself slipping into one, then pulling on stockings and shoes, then buttoning up the fur coat, then tying a scarf around my mouth to mask my face, and striding across the lobby, past the curious concierge, into the frigid New York night. The blood began banging in my ears. I had to sit down on the edge of the bed. What was I so afraid of? The cold? The hubbub? The stares? Negotiating an icy curb? Getting lost in my own hometown? Or was I afraid that the moment I stepped outside I would feel at home here, and then what would all those years on Ta'un'uu have meant?

I shut the closet, then picked up the note with Alice's number on it. I needed to talk to someone who knew me as I once was. I wanted to tell her how sorry I was about Julien, wanted her to know that Philip had died, too. I pushed the buttons on the telephone and heard unearthly, musical tones, then the drone of a ringing line.

A hoarse, shaky voice answered, "Hello? Hello? Who's there?"

The voice sounded so old, I hung up.

The phone book sat next to the phone. I started turning pages. Had the print gotten so much smaller or the city so much larger? I wasn't even sure who I was looking for. I simply needed to know who was still alive. I ran my finger down a column until I thought I recognized a name. Alex Auffenberg. Wasn't he the Dadaist poet who wrote without ink in his pen? What would I say to him if it really turned out to be him, if the old poet picked up the phone? Are you still writing? Or would I just hang up on him as I had Alice? What had prompted me to come back at my age?

I opened the wet bar. Miniature bottles lined the shelves. Bourbon. Brandy. Vodka. Scotch. Rye. Cognac. Why switch now? I uncapped the Hennessy, drank it right from the spout. Aside from the hum of the little refrigerator and the thumping pulse of my irrepressible existence, the suite was tomb-silent. I'd forgotten how deafening an empty room can be. I turned on what I thought was a radio in a big wooden cabinet, just for the company, and a moving picture appeared. In color. A close-up of a pretty actress. I watched with complete fascination. They'd found a way to bring motion pictures into the home. They'd sent a man to the moon. What other wonders have they come up with? The actress touched her fingers to her temples in the universal gesture for "I can't go on." It turned out to be an advertisement for Bayer aspirin. I turned off the picture and stared at the glass screen, a mirror really. I switched on a lamp and picked up the *Life* magazine. I so needed to be with people who know me as I am now. The table of contents read *Mrs.*

Crusoe Among a Lost South Seas Tribe. I opened to a centerfold of the Great Tapestry. Even without the natural billowing of swaying bodies to animate the design, it looked remarkable, exquisite. I'm the only one on Ta'un'uu who has ever witnessed the full display of the Great Tapestry from without. I must ask *Life* for enough copies to bring back with me as gifts.

I turned the page to a photographic montage of island life—gardening, fishing, feasting, the final shot, a portrait of the elders. Cast in the light of an incandescent bulb, they look so very far away. I tried to imagine my return, the Great Tapestry coming apart as everyone runs to greet me, as everyone insists on pressing their forehead against mine. A sow will be sacrificed and sung about, then eaten. The youngsters will all want tattoos from my world. But after a day or two, the village will return to its old routine as if none of this had ever happened, and my world will once again fold shut.

What if I don't want to go back? What if I choose to stay? It's not entirely outside the realm of possibility. It's not as if I have to make a decision tonight. I'm not foolish enough to think that I even know where I am . . . but still. *Life* must have a contingency plan in case I should ask to stay. They could hardly just abandon me. They'd be under some obligation to help, if not legally, at least in the public's eye. Perhaps I could parlay my notoriety into a modest living for a time? One of my paintings is, after all, hanging in the Modern. Alice might even know a gallery dealer willing to set me up in a small studio, nothing special, a garret, say, in the Village. The Village wouldn't be as frightening as Midtown. I could take up painting again. Unlike skin, one never runs out of canvas. Eventually, I would feel at home here. I came to feel at home on

Ta'un'uu, didn't I? What would my days be like? Wake up early to a wintry dawn. Fix myself a cup of coffee with two teaspoons of sugar and real cream. Sip it while opening my paints. I could still call up the smell of turpentine. I would lunch out at a coffee shop, Chock full o'Nuts if need be. I'd buy my smokes at a newspaper kiosk, perhaps even flirt with the old guy inside. "Hey Mrs. E., got your picture in the paper lately?" "Not lately," I'd say.

Then, one afternoon, I'd fail to show up for my cigarettes, and someone would be sent to my door only to find me cold and dead in a crypt-silent studio. I'd rank a photograph with my obituary. How could they not include a picture of *my* face? And perhaps a retrospective at a museum. I'd be buried beside my mother and father in the city of coffins with nobody to remove my skin, my art, before I have to face all my dead loved ones.

I looked up from my copy of *Life.* Staring back at me from the center of the glass-radio-motion-picture-screen—backlit, ethereal—sat an old tattooed ghost in a hotel robe.

Brooke rapped on my door first thing the next morning.

I was just finishing breakfast—coffee with real cream and two sugars, a one-minute egg, another scrambled with lox, and a bagel with cream cheese. And I'd managed to get myself into a dress. In the light of day, the task hadn't seemed so formidable. I'd even put on silk stockings. They'd done away with girdles! But when I'd tried to slip on shoes, I couldn't make myself do it. It was as if last night's panic now resided in a pair of shoes. If I put them on, I would put on the panic itself.

"May I come in? Did you sleep well?" Brooke asked, looking around to see how I'd spent my first night. Was the wet bar open? Was the wet bar empty? Had I discovered the motion-picture machine? Did I forgo the pillows? Did I sleep on the floor? She noticed my stocking feet.

"I couldn't find any shoes that fit," I lied.

She headed for the closet, brought back a pair of brown oxfords, knelt before me, eased my feet into them, laced them up, then had me stand and take a few steps. I could no longer feel the world underfoot. I walked over to the window.

"How do they feel?"

With my back to her, I pretended to test the fit, but all I really wanted was a moment of privacy to comprehend *and* appreciate the impossible fact that I was wearing shoes again.

"Are they comfortable?"

"They'll do."

She came up behind me, offered me a Chesterfield, then lit one for herself. "You must have thought about what you want to do while you're here, Sara. Who you'd like to visit? Would you like to start by seeing your painting at the Modern?"

I closed my eyes for a moment, but try as I did, I could no more envision *Self-Portrait Without Vanishing Point* than I could the dead's faces. "I'd prefer to wait to see my old work," I said, "until I'm a little more used to the present."

"Of course." She took another puff of her cigarette, then left it to smolder away in an ashtray. "Would you like to just drive around for a while, Sara? Orient yourself? We could go to the top of the Empire State Building, let you get a bird's-eye view of all the changes that have taken place."

"I've never been," I admitted.

She smiled. "Neither have I. Shall we?"

"Would you give me a moment," I said.

"Take all the time you need. I'll be waiting in the lobby with Jack." She shut the door behind her. I slipped the fur coat on, then retrieved the hat, gloves, and scarf left for me on the vanity. I set the hat atop my white hair, buttoned up my coat, then pulled on the gloves. It took a rattled moment or two for me to grasp what I saw in the center panel of the vanity's mirror: my mother, dressed as she had always dreamed, in a fur coat from Saks. Ishmael's black had faded over the years, but the line was as commanding as ever.

Would I face New York masked or unmasked? I left the scarf on the vanity.

Brooke, Jack, and I shared an elevator up to the eighty-sixth floor of the Empire State Building with a tour group from Kansas and a guide who seemed beside himself that he might appear in *Life*. When he thought no one was looking, he primped in the elevator's mirrored panel.

We exited as a group and were herded onto a blowing, snowy deck. For a moment, everyone fell mute, dumbstruck by the view. New York no longer looked like a mere island metropolis from up here, it looked like a man-made cosmos. As far as the eye could see, human enterprise and edifices. Planes crossed the sky, ships the harbor. Horns, clanging steel, and human clamor rose out of the grid of streets, borne on icy updrafts. How had I believed, even for only a minute or two last night, that I could make my way out there? Where do the old people rest?

As soon as the initial awe had passed, and the tourists had

taken their pictures of the view, I noticed a few of the cameras stray my way.

"Opening day, when Governor-soon-to-be-President Roosevelt stood where you're standing now," the guide intoned, "he said, 'I've got an entirely new conception of things in the city of New York!'"

I overheard one lady whisper to her husband, "Do you think they rub off?"

"Built in nineteen-thirty-one, out of fifty-seven tons of steel, at a cost of forty-one million—that's ninety-eight million in today's dollars—the Empire State Building is still the tallest building in the world. We are standing twelve hundred and fifty feet above Fifth Avenue, atop two million square feet of office space. If you'll look up, you can see another two hundred and twenty-two feet of television antenna added in nineteen-fifty at an additional cost of four-point-eight million. To our north is Rockefeller Center. Its base takes up sixteen square blocks of the most valuable real estate in the world . . ."

The guide was shouting out New York's history, *my* history, as dollars and change. As the crowd pressed against the balustrade to get a better view of the world's most pricey acreage, I ventured up to the snowy edge, too. From this omnipotent height, Rockefeller Plaza didn't appear much bigger than a tiny vale in a mountain range. Philip, Alice, and Julien, our comrades from the Artists' Union, the sad Jewish couple with their horror tales from Germany, even Diego Rivera himself must have looked so infinitesimal marching down Fifth Avenue with our little red banners of protest to anyone standing on the observation deck that day.

"Oh my God, Sara, you must be freezing!" Brooke said, staring aghast at my shoes.

I looked down. I was ankle-deep in snow melt. I couldn't sense whether my shoes had taken on ice water, or whether my dead loved ones had finally gotten ahold of my feet.

"The oxfords don't seem to be waterproof," I said.

I was immediately chauffeured to Saks Fifth Avenue to pick out a new pair of shoes, boots if I preferred, and warm heavy socks. The department manager himself welcomed me to Saks's shoe "gallery," then escorted me through the exhibits—a pair of gold lamé high heels pedestaled on a sculpture stand, a single red thigh-high boot lit by a hot white spotlight, a salon-style presentation of pointy-toed flats made from every imaginable animal skin. He had me sit down on a chair so that he could personally measure my feet for a proper fit.

Behind bins of sale shoes, carousels of stockings, shoppers stared at me. Undoing my frozen laces, he helped me out of the wet oxfords, then placed my chilled foot onto a measuring implement, the same kind they'd used when I was a girl. I'd grown one full size and widened to a triple E. Apologizing that Saks didn't carry a fuller selection in my size, he went to see what he could find.

Two teenage girls wandered by, so engrossed in the extravaganza of footwear that they failed to notice the old, cold tattooed feet sharing the aisle.

The department manager returned with a short stack of boxes. "Let's see if one of these has your name on it," he said. Opening the top lid, he took out a pair of fleece-lined, square-toed ankle boots, then slipped them on my feet. "It's one of our most popular styles this winter. Very comfortable and very warm. It also comes in dark brown, burgundy, and black."

Jack's camera whirred and clicked.

"Do you like them?" Brooke asked.

Nothing rubbed, nothing pinched. They seemed fine, perfectly adequate. I rose to test the fit, but it wasn't necessary: five minutes in the company of all this bounty and the remarkableness of wearing shoes again was gone.

"I'll take them," I said.

"You don't want to try on *any* others?" Brooke asked, shaking her head in wonder. "I can't go three days without shopping, Sara. How did you manage thirty years?"

The manager started to put my old oxfords into a shopping bag, but Brooke whispered, "No." He discreetly dropped them into a trash pail behind the counter. It took everything in my power not to retrieve them.

"Would you like to look around Saks a little longer?" Brooke asked. "You could choose gifts for everyone back home." She drew my attention to a display of iridescent scarves: the dyes looked as if they'd been mixed with neon. I'd never seen color like that before.

"If I picked one out for the chief's wife," Brooke asked, "would you give it to her for me when you get home, Sara?"

So it never crossed her mind that I might not go back, that after my two weeks were up, after *Life* had wined and dined me, I might not be able to return to an islet in the middle of the ocean where a pair of shoes is treasured for generations.

"Perhaps we can shop for gifts later," I said, but I didn't promise to bring the scarf back with me.

Saks's front doors sprang open without my even touching them. Fresh snow powdered the sidewalk. Brooke, Jack, and I hurried into the warm, waiting limousine. Only when the line of taxis behind us wouldn't quit honking did it occur to me that the reason we weren't moving was that everyone was waiting for me to tell the chauffeur where *I* wanted to go.

"There must be some special place you'd like to see again?" Brooke asked, ignoring the horns.

Philip's and my house on Washington Mews? The tenement I grew up in? My parents' graves? I couldn't bear to visit the city of coffins on my very first day back. "I'm not used to so many options," I said. "Is there someplace I could just sit quietly and watch?"

"Watch?" She thought for a moment. "Would you like to see the moon landing? *Life* has a private screening room. It's about as quiet as New York gets, and you can just sit and watch."

"They made a newsreel of the moon landing?"

"Sara, the whole world watched from their living rooms." She tapped on the chauffeur's partition. "Downtown. Take the West Side, it's faster at this hour."

Somewhere on Tenth Avenue near Pennsylvania Station, I spotted a tattoo parlor shoehorned between two peep show theaters.

"I'd like to stop," I said.

"It's not a safe neighborhood," Brooke cautioned, as if naked breasts and tattoos would intimidate me at this late juncture in my journey.

"Just for a minute," I said.

The proprietor, twenty years my junior, and almost as tattooed, glanced up from a barber chair in which he was napping. "No photographs," he warned Jack. Then he blinked at my face, my silk-stockinged legs, the designs on my throat, the exposed swatch of skin between my gloved wrists and my fur cuffs, then at my face again. "All hand done?" he asked.

"Yes."

The wall behind him was papered with skulls, serpents, hula girls, chutes-and-boots, a "tea" leaf, a mushroom, a raised fist, MOM, DEATH, SAT CONG, FUCK WAR, American flags.

"Would it be all right if I looked around?"

He stood, making way for me, all the while studying Ishmael's work on my face. An electric needle hung from a hook, attached to a motor by a long, black cable.

"I've never seen one in action before," I said.

He demonstrated it for me by tattooing a line on an orange rind. The motor was so loud, I thought, he must not be able to hear himself singing.

"May I see?" I asked, pointing to his forearm. He rolled up his sleeve for me. NO REMORSE was tattooed on the biceps.

"I'd do you one for free," he said as I turned to leave, "but it looks as if your dance card is already full."

In a dark, two-row theater, along with Brooke, Jack, and Brooke's editor, a very tall, very concave gentleman, I watched a spaceman climb down a gangplank and set one foot, then the other, on the moon. In a voice breaking apart with reverence and static, he said something I couldn't make out.

"Incredible, isn't it?" the editor said. "Would you like to see and hear it again, Mrs. Ehrenreich? We can rewind the tape."

"I'd like to keep going," I said.

At three paces, the spaceman turned around to face what must have been a camera mounted on his rocket ship. I couldn't read his expression. His visage was a mirror. Reflected in it, a tiny blue and green earth rose over the moon's horizon. I couldn't quite believe that I was seeing home from such a wondrous, unthinkable distance. He must have been as dumbstruck as I, and as terrified. More than anyone on earth, he must have considered what would happen if he became marooned up there, if he had to live out what remained of his life in such an alien world. I watched with apprehension until he and his two companions were safe on earth again, bobbing on a piece of their spaceship in the middle of the ocean. I so hoped a ship would rescue them soon.

The lights came on. I was back. Here. Wherever here was.

"It's a little after one o'clock," Brooke said as she climbed into the limousine behind me. "Where would you like to go for lunch, Sara? A lot of the old restaurants are still around."

I tried to remember where Philip and I, in our better days, used to have lunch, but an earlier memory begged my attention: my father and I sharing a sandwich at Katz's. Why was the promise of food so invariably tethered to the wrench of childhood nostalgia?

"Is Katz's still around?" I asked.

"I think so," Brooke said. "Do you know where it is?" she asked the driver.

"On Ludlow and Houston," I said.

The decor hadn't changed. Aged salamis still hung from hooks, perhaps the very same salamis that had hung when I was a girl. Most of the patrons looked as old as me.

The woman manning the cash register pointed me out to her customer, and a moment later the whole restaurant was gaping at me over their half-eaten sandwiches. Finally, a counterman shouted to his hard-of-hearing customers, "That's Mrs.

Ehrenreich, the tattooed lady from *Life*. Am I right, Mrs. Ehrenreich?"

I nodded, and everyone resumed eating.

"What can I get you today?" he asked.

"I'd like a pastrami on rye with mustard," I said.

He speared a hunk of pastrami from a steaming pot, carved off a portion, then fixed me an impossibly thick sandwich, slavering the top slice with mustard. *"Du vilst essen a zour* pickle *mit unst?"*

"Half-sour, please."

I ferried my sandwich to an empty table. Brooke ordered soup, then sat opposite me. Jack reloaded his camera.

"Put the camera away," I said. "I'm eating." But I didn't touch my sandwich. I kept looking around at the other diners. There must be old union boys and girls among them, if not from my Waist Makers' Union, then from the Buttonhole Makers' Union. That wizened thing at the next table might have run the sewing machine beside mine, she might have shared a bench with me in Washington Square. She looked so stubbornly familiar. Even if she didn't know me, she might still recognize me as the counterman had, as a long-lost member of the tribe.

"Is something wrong with your sandwich?" Brooke asked at last.

"It's a little more challenging to eat then I remember," I said, lifting up the heavy brick of pastrami. I took a small, messy bite, then wiped my tattooed lips with a paper napkin. The busboys let loose Bronx whistles. Despite the racket, I overheard the old shopgirl whisper to her friend, "They'll never allow her to be buried as a Jew."

. . .

The temperature had dropped again by the time we left, or perhaps it only felt like that after the torpid heat of Katz's. We dashed into the waiting limousine.

"How're you holding up?" Brooke asked, glancing at her watch as she slid in behind me. It flashed 2:14. Watches no longer had faces. "We still have the whole afternoon, Sara. Would you like to go to the Met, or the galleries?"

Was it only two o'clock in the afternoon? We hadn't been driving around for days, weeks, months, just a handful of hours? "I must lie down," I said, "I'm exhausted."

"The Waldorf," she told the driver. "Sara, I'm sorry. How thoughtless of me. You must be so overwhelmed. And on top of everything, you have jet lag."

"I've never heard the term," I said.

"It means your body's clock is still on island time. It's early dawn in the village. You'd just be waking up."

For a fraction of a second, Schimmel's Knishes, Russ & Daughters Smoked Fish, the Yiddish newspaper stand, the bus, the endless torrents of yellow taxis were blotted out by a particularly tender pink tropical dawn.

"There's a fifteen-hour difference between Ta'un'uu and New York," she added.

I waited for the irony of what Brooke had just said to occur to her, but her face remained as innocent as ever. Did she actually believe fifteen hours could register beside thirty years?

I fell asleep on top of the covers, too tired to undress, though I managed to pull off my new boots. When I finally awoke, I raised my head to see where in the world I was. In which hemisphere? On what island? The window was dark. The skyline had been extinguished while I'd been sleeping. It was the middle of the night, and here I was, once again, fully, mercilessly wide awake in an empty hotel room with nothing but panic for company.

What a foolish old woman I was to have come back after all this time, no different from any other sentimental old immigrant spending her last wish to see home again. Wasn't it better that my father never got to witness what had become of his little singing *yeshiva* on the Russian steppes?

I turned on the light. In the mirror opposite the bed, I saw the bottom of my tattooed feet. I'd never before seen them from such a fresh, unimaginable angle. Etched in raw umber on my right sole was my empty, open coffin, and on my left, in red oxide, was Philip's closed one. I'd always meant for them to be viewed as a diptych. When I leave here, I'll never get to see them again. Not from this angle. Wasn't that alone worth the journey? Maybe I should go home right now. Really, what else is left for me to see here? Alice? She's in her late eighties. Why make her suffer an appearance from a ghost. My parents' graves? I never bothered when I lived here. The newest technology? I'd already witnessed a man on the moon. My old painting hanging in the Modern? I couldn't even remember what it looked like.

If I could have gotten into the museum then and there, I would have run the five blocks in my bare feet, on my tattooed coffins. How could I go home without seeing my old work?

I waited for the sun to break over the rooftops before putting on my hat and coat. In the elevator, I wound my scarf around my face until only my eyes were visible. I so needed this to be a private viewing.

I walked the icy sidewalks to Fifth Avenue. The museum used to be in the old Heckscher Building, up on the twelfth floor, but according to the young doorman, those suites were now a law firm. He pointed me four blocks south. Tilting into the wind, I trudged to the corner of Fifty-third. When I finally reached the museum's glass entrance, the guard wouldn't let me inside. The museum didn't open for another two hours.

Across the street, in a steamy window, a neon sign promised HOT COFFEE, HOT DOUGHNUTS, HOT BAGELS. I got as far as the coffee shop door before it occurred to me that I was penniless. *Life* hadn't given me any spending money, and I had forgotten to ask. I hadn't given money a thought in three decades.

I couldn't remain outdoors much longer. Where do the penniless go to keep warm? I walked to Grand Central and pushed open the doors against a tide of commuters. The pace was dizzying. More people were arriving by train. I needed to sit down, but every bench I approached was already occupied by the penniless. No one cared to move over for a lady in a fur coat.

I fled by the south entrance. A sign in the window of a bar across the street read OPEN. The sign looked older than me. I wove between bumpers frozen at a red light and stepped inside. The only other customer was asleep, his cheek on the counter. The old proprietress was washing a glass. She studied me curiously, but it wasn't my face that piqued her interest. The scarf was still in place. It was the fur coat in her establishment at eight-thirty in the morning.

I took a seat at the bar. "Hennessy, a double please," I said. I pulled off my gloves, then unwound the scarf from around my mouth and throat. I thought she was going to drop the cognac bottle, but she managed to pour me a shot without taking her eyes off my face. She didn't appear to recognize me, though. I guess her *Life* subscription had lapsed a long time ago.

"I haven't got any money," I said.

She filled up my glass to the brim anyway. "Honey, I don't know what your story is, but you look like you've earned this drink."

Slightly tipsy, I stood outside the museum. The doors were now open, but there was an admission fee. Fifty cents for seniors. A tour group of Upper East Side ladies was being ushered through the entrance by a shivering docent. No one noticed the extra fur coat. Near the coat-check room, in a glass information booth, sat an officious-looking young woman.

"Could you help me?" I asked. "Where are your paintings from the nineteen-twenties?"

"The Early Modernists?" She pointed me toward the escalators. "Second floor, make a left when you see the Brillo boxes, go straight past Abstract Expressionism, through the double doors—you'll be in the nineteen-thirties—make another sharp left at Surrealism, and that's where you'll find the early part of the century." She looked at my scarf, then down at my heavy fur. "We have a coat check if you'd like," she added.

At the top of the escalator, just where she said they would be, Brillo boxes were stacked three high. I couldn't tell if the museum now allowed advertising or if they were part of the exhibit. Perhaps the Ta'un'uuans were right after all to covet the beauty of the cargo shells? Perhaps the shells themselves are the gift? On the wall behind them hung a billboard-sized painting of a little girl helmeted in a hair dryer, piloting a rocket ship through spaghetti. A guard was standing next to a drawing of a two-dollar bill. The title read, *Two-Dollar Bill with Jefferson*.

"The Early Modernists?" I asked.

He pointed me toward the corridor. "Make a sharp left."

"Thank you," I said. When I made the sharp left, I found myself in another room of billboard-sized canvases, but unlike the little girl rocketing through spaghetti, these canvases were alive with raging forces, slashes of pigment, drips of color. The drip was such a poignant way to create a living line. I wondered if I could do something like that with ink on skin.

I tried the next gallery. *American Gothic. Tornadoes in the Heartland.* A Ben Shahn. A Diego Rivera. All Philip's and my old friends and enemies hanging side by side—the Regionalist shared a spotlight with the Social Realist, the Anarchists flanked the Trotskyite, the Stalinist hung beside the Fascist—and all were beautifully framed and owned by the same private collectors.

And then I saw my own painting, center wall between O'Keeffe and Man Ray, a naked young woman—me—supine under a night sky, on a tar roof. I'd framed the canvas in an old tenement window sash, set it under a cracked yellow pane, and painted the roof with real tar. The young woman's face was turned so that her eyes stared directly at the viewer: her pupils were swirls of zealous, adamant, unrelenting hope. Above her pristine body, isolated on moonlit clouds, rose utopias run by perpetual motion machines. I must have used too much medium in those days, or not enough, because my surface, unlike the other Early Modernists, was already rent with tiny cracks.

I stepped closer and tried to look directly into the eyes of the young woman I was some fifty years ago, but she wouldn't look at me. She stared past me, through me, preoccupied, oblivious to what was standing right before her. When I'd painted those eyes, I'd intended that the naked Eve appear to be transfixed by what the viewer can't yet see, a future in which every shopgirl gets to drink from her boss's crystal, but what I'd really captured in those cracking, trustful eyes was me staring at my own mortality.

I read the wall text: *SELF-PORTRAIT WITHOUT VANISHING POINT, 1923.* SARA EHRENREICH (1902–39).

The Ta'un'uuans always reserve a small patch of virgin skin, unsoiled by the needle, for any last images, any final words, so to speak, before the canvas has been completely saturated with one's exploits. The patch is always on the palm, left if you're right-handed, and vice versa. It's understood by the islanders that even those unskilled with the needle, the clumsiest fisherman, say, will want to put the final touches on their story with their own hand. For a tattoo artist like myself, it's expected.

I press zero for the Waldorf's front desk and ask that a sewing kit with a wide assortment of needles be brought to my suite.

The last tattoo shouldn't be more revered than any other tattoo, but how could it not be? It's the final tattoo to be removed before the body journeys to the afterworld, the last image of vanity to be fed to the fishes.

A chambermaid arrives a few minutes later with a wide assortment of threads, but only one needle. I tip her anyway with an armful of my brand-new dresses, then shut the door behind her. I inspect the needle, hold it up to the light. The shaft is slightly bent, but the point looks solid and sharp. It will have to do.

I pick up a ballpoint pen, unscrew the plastic halves, and remove the vein of ink. Breaking off one end, I squeeze the liquid out into a glass ashtray. It's a lovely dark color, though by no means as rich and complex as the black I mix at home.

I strike a match to sterilize the needle's tip, then dip the red-hot point into the waiting ink.

The image I tattoo is very simple—forty pricks at most. If one doesn't know the whole story behind it, it looks like an upside-down T or a crude anchor or an unfinished cross, the blunder of an old tattoo artist's diminishing talents, when in fact it's a simple stick figure atop a tiny stick raft trying to navigate a course home across my open hand.

ACKNOWLEDGMENTS

Though *The Tattoo Artist* is a work of fiction, I am indebted to the following sources for research and guidance:

A Bintel Brief: Sixty Years, edited by Isaac Metzker

Cargo Cult: Strange Stories of Desire from Melanesia and Beyond, by Lamont Lindstrom

Oceanic Art, by Nicolas Thomas

Primitive Art, by Franz Boas

Road Belong Cargo: A Study of the Cargo Movement in the Southern Madang District, New Guinea, by Peter Lawrence

Strange Bedfellows: The First American Avant-Garde, by Steven Watson

World of Our Fathers: The Journey of the East European Jews to America and the Life They Found and Made, by Irving Howe

Wrapping in Images: Tattooing in Polynesia, by Alfred Gell

Written on the Body: The Tattoo in European and American History, edited by Jane Caplan

ACKNOWLEDGMENTS

I am grateful to Jo Ann Beard, Lisa Cohen, Bernard Cooper, Amy Hempel, A. M. Homes, David Leavitt, Arnold Mesches, Lisa Michaels, Mark Mitchell, Ann Patty, and Sam Swope for their patience, suggestions, and contributions.

I especially want to thank Gail Hochman and Vicky Wilson for their generous support.

I also wish to thank the New York State Foundation for the Arts.

ACT OF GOD

It's the summer of 2015, Brooklyn, and the city is sweltering from another record-breaking heat wave, this one accompanied by biblical rains. Edith, a recently retired legal librarian, and her identical twin sister, Kat, have discovered something ominous in their hall closet: it's shaped like a mushroom, it's phosphorescent, and it's rapidly consuming their wall. But that's only the beginning. . . . Part suspense, part screwball comedy, Jill Ciment's brilliant novel looks at what happens when our lives—so seemingly set and ordered—break down in the wake of calamity.

Fiction

HEROIC MEASURES

New York City is on high alert—a gasoline truck is "stuck" in the Midtown tunnel and the driver has fled. Through panic and gridlock, Alex and Ruth must transport their dachshund—whose back legs are suddenly paralyzed—to the animal hospital. But this is also the weekend when Alex and Ruth must sell the apartment in which they have lived for most of their adult lives. Over the course of forty-eight hours, as the mystery of the missing driver terrorizes the city and the dachshund's life hangs in the balance, the bidding war over their apartment becomes a barometer for hope and despair. *Heroic Measures* is a moving, deft novel about urban anxiety and the love that deepens over years.

Fiction